| DATE DUE | | | |
|---|---|---|---|
| MAY 0 3 1996 | | | |
| MAY 2 1 1996 | | | |
| OCT 1 0 1997 | | | |
| | | | |
| | | | |
| | | | |
| | | | |
| | | | |
| | | | |
| | | | |
| | | | |
| | | | |

F
And     Anderson, Mary
        The Unsinkable Molly
        Malone

GAYLORD M2

# The Unsinkable Molly Malone

*Mademoiselle Charlotte du Val d'Ognes*

# The Unsinkable Molly Malone

### Mary Anderson

HARCOURT BRACE JOVANOVICH, PUBLISHERS
SAN DIEGO   NEW YORK   LONDON

Library of Congress Cataloging-in-Publication Data
Anderson, Mary, 1929–
The unsinkable Molly Malone/by Mary Anderson.
p.   cm.
Summary: Sixteen-year-old Molly, a socially conscious, struggling
artist living in New York, befriends a group of children living in a
welfare hotel and, incidentally, falls in love with a mysterious
young man.
ISBN 0-15-213801-3
[1. Artists—Fiction.   2. Interpersonal relations—Fiction.
3. Homeless persons—Fiction.   4. New York (N.Y.)—Fiction.]
I. Title.
PZ7.A5444Un   1991
[Fic]—dc20      91-10967

Designed by Lisa Peters

Printed in the United States of America
First edition          A B C D E

*Frontispiece*: French Painter, Unknown. Portrait of a Young Woman,
called Mademoiselle Charlotte du Val d'Ognes. The Metropolitan Museum
of Art, Bequest of Isaac D. Fletcher, 1917. Mr. and Mrs. Isaac D. Fletcher
Collection. Copyright © 1981 by the Metropolitan Museum of Art.

# The Unsinkable Molly Malone

# One

When the history of the world is written—that final chapter (which could be any day considering how fast we're fouling up this planet)—I think I know what the sum total of human knowledge will mean.

Don't count on anyone!

Isaac called to break it off—officially, that is. I already knew we were finished. It happened because of our disagreement (which he called an argument) about his senior prom. But I consider two opposing opinions a disagreement, don't you? Not Isaac. You should've heard him!

We were sitting in Angela's Coffee Shop, and Isaac was refusing to go along with my suggestion.

"Come off it, Molly, I've already rented the tux. I've

put down my deposit on the dinner and everything. Why should I trash all that?"

"For a principle," I told him. "Kids spend a fortune on their senior prom dinner dance, but they're usually too drunk to taste the food. It's such a waste, Isaac. If you donate that dinner money to a soup kitchen or the Salvation Army you'd all graduate feeling great. Don't you get it?"

"I guess not," he said. "I'll only graduate from Stuyvesant once, and the prom symbolizes something. It's important."

"That's the point," I told him. "That's why you should make this meaningful gesture. You're the class president, Isaac. If you vote for this, the other kids will go along."

As I watched him stare into his overpriced coffee, I knew I'd made him real uncomfortable.

"You don't know most of the kids in my class. They all want one last good time before starting college," he insisted. "You will, too, Molly. Just wait until you graduate next year."

"I don't think so," I told him. "In fact, I wouldn't be caught dead spending money on my prom."

"Then maybe you shouldn't be caught dead at mine, either!" he shouted.

Then he left.

Needless to say, I didn't go to Isaac's prom. He took Millicent Duggan instead. That's ironic. Millicent's father could pay off the national debt with what she squanders on overpriced clothes. Not only did he refuse to donate his dinner to charity, he took that clotheshorse to the prom—totally canceling out whatever social statement my absence might have made.

The day after the prom, Isaac called me. Early in the morning. With a hangover and lots of opinions. And that's when he informed me we weren't "suited" for each other.

I agreed.

That made him angry. "Know what you are, Molly? You're a throwback! That's right, a throwback to that hippie, Sixties, love-beads generation. Know what happened to those do-gooders? They all blew their minds on drugs and wound up on the trash heap!"

Charming, eh? And after we'd gone together for three months. "Have a nice life, Isaac," I said sweetly. "A nice uncommitted, uninvolved, no-hassle life," I added, slamming down the receiver.

I felt rotten the minute I'd said it. So I went into the M.R.

I once saw an actor being interviewed on TV who said, "Acting is the place I go." That's exactly how I feel about art. Art is the place I go when I'm feeling good or bad or even when I'm not feeling anything. And all my art is produced in my workroom, the M.R.

Mom and I live in an old building on Riverside Drive in New York City that was built at the turn of the century when they still made *real* walls and strong floors. You can't hear your neighbors, not even if they're killing each other. There are built-in buttons by the doors (long since painted over) to summon the servants, and a gizmo in the dining-room floor, which does the same thing. Of course, every apartment has a maid's room. Even though there aren't any maids living in them anymore, they're still called maid's rooms. Everyone knows an M.R. means the smallest room in the apartment with an adjoining bath.

But for me, M.R. means my studio. Mom calls it the trash heap, the nightmare, the wreck, the rotting retreat, or the place that time forgot. I guess it's all those things, but it's also all mine, my lifetime of collecting garbage.

Mom doesn't dare set foot inside—not that she'd want to, I collect too many strange objects. Once I kept a squashed mouse that had been run over several times. It looked fabulous lying there, just like an etching in the street. I couldn't resist it, so I took it home. I tried to preserve it by spraying it with fixative, then by freezing. Neither worked, so I finally had to throw it out. Now, I have every kind of trash (except for dead things) tucked away somewhere. Only I don't think of it as trash. To me, it's all found treasure to use in my artwork.

I'm very organized. Everything is cataloged. The printer's drawers I found on the street hold the bigger things. I use garbage as containers for garbage. Artistic symmetry, I call it.

Mom still calls it a disgusting mess. Sometimes that makes me feel guilty, because if I weren't using the space she could rent out the M.R. Since our apartment is rent controlled, we could practically live rent-free on what she could get from a tenant in that dinky room, only I couldn't bear to part with it. Mom's piano lessons

4

pay our basic monthly bills, but I need to sell enough artwork each month to pay my share of the expenses. It would break my heart to lose my work space.

Isaac's phone call had made me feel totally rotten; I needed to deal with my feelings, so as usual I put them into my work. It was still morning, so I had enough time before I started selling outside the Metropolitan Museum on Fifth Avenue. I usually don't arrive there until noon, when the crowds start coming.

In my collection of old *Playbill* magazines, I found one from a Sixties off-Broadway show called *The Last Sweet Days of Isaac*. Perfect! I ripped off the cover and began my collage. Beside the *Playbill*, I glued down some wooden coffee stirrers (Isaac loves gourmet coffee), some pop-top lids (he's addicted to diet soda), old shoelaces (he jogs), and some dried monarch butterfly wings and seashells we'd found together on the beach. Using my glue gun, I arranged them beside a broken leather watchband (Isaac is a schedule freak), near a birthday card Isaac had sent me. I also included a dried fish spine (my ironic touch, since I actually consider Isaac spineless!). To this arrangement I added various bits and pieces, including some dried-up fruit peels to represent Isaac's desiccated personality.

When I'd finished, I felt much better.

I dragged out my hand truck and began to load it up. After stacking my card table, my folding chair, my jewelry cases, portfolio and the art supplies I'd use later, I was all set for a day's work.

I hadn't counted on Mom lying in wait for me in the living room. She was on the sofa reading the paper, and she peered over it as I dragged my hand truck across the room. I could tell by her eyes I was in for trouble!

"Mr. and Mrs. Lenahan of Manhattan announce the engagement of their daughter, Marcie, to Joseph Witherspoon of Brownsville," Mom read. She stared at me as if this was highly significant, then looked back at her paper. "Joseph Witherspoon is presently a law student at Harvard."

"Terrific, Mom," I said. "Never heard of them, but that's terrific."

"I'm glad you think so," she said coolly. "Isaac will be a lawyer someday, too, and it's too bad you'll never hear sweet words like that. He would've been a great catch, Molly. But you had to go and ruin everything. A young man's high school graduation comes only once, you know."

"That's what he told me."

"How could you crush his hopes?"

I had to laugh. "Isaac didn't waste time finding someone else. He had his hot hands on Millicent Duggan right away!"

"Don't be crude," Mom scolded, "that was only on the rebound."

Sometimes I think Mom would like to live in a world created by Tennessee Williams, a world populated by "beaux" and "gentlemen callers." She even looks a little like one of Williams's slightly faded beauties. But my dad had the real good looks. Too handsome for his own good, Mom always said.

"Isaac never would have dropped you if you had behaved properly," Mom added.

6

I was too busy to argue the point. It was Saturday, my biggest sale day, so I wanted to get over to Fifth Avenue before my favorite spot was taken.

"And I'm sure he had a miserable time at the prom without you," she added.

"Don't worry," I assured her, "I'll bet he got lucky with Millicent."

Mom looked offended. "Such bad manners. I have no idea where you acquired them, Molly. Certainly not from *me*; I was brought up to value manners."

All my arguments with Mom are strictly the knee-jerk variety: we push each other's buttons, and then we're off. "The biggest hypocrites in the world hide behind good manners, Mom. You told me Dad had great manners—always walking on the outside of the sidewalk and junk like that. So what?"

"Don't speak ill of the dead," Mom snapped. "You know your poor father died all alone—a stranger in a strange place."

Whenever Mom brings up how Dad died, she takes all the fun out of fighting. That "stranger in a strange place" stuff is strictly something Mom made up to tell people. But she's said it so often, maybe she believes it now. The truth is, Dad died when I was six. Besides having perfect manners, he was a perfect con man, an incurable gambler, and an alcoholic. He died somewhere in Canada, on his way to a racetrack to bet money he didn't have on a horse that probably didn't win. He had been drinking too much and suffered a heart attack. Those are the pathetic facts.

I dragged my hand truck toward the door. "It's been fun. Let's fight again tonight, okay?"

Mom grinned, in spite of herself. "Glib. You're always so glib, Molly Malone. What time will you be home?"

"About eight."

"Are you going to that dreadful place again?"

I teased her. "The Metropolitan Museum of Art isn't dreadful."

"I mean that *other* place. That awful welfare hotel."

"Sure. I always go on Saturday."

"Be careful."

"Should I pick up some dinner?"

"I think there's half a roast left."

"Maybe I'll get some Chinese. How many students do you have today?"

"Only seven today. My ten o'clock is sick, so her mom canceled. Freddie Sumner is my last, at six o'clock."

I groaned. "Air out this place before I get back, okay? Freddie always farts during his lesson."

"Shame on you, Molly. Can't you ever be serious?"

"Who me? Not Molly Malone."

Mom went over to the piano and began to play. "I named you properly. I guess I always knew my little girl would grow up to be a street vendor."

Mom started singing.

> *"In Dublin's fair city*
> *Where the girls are so pretty*
> *Twas there I first met her*
> *Sweet Molly Malone*
>
> *And she wheeled her wheelbarrow*
> *Through streets broad and narrow . . ."*

I went into the kitchen. "Quit kidding," I shouted, opening the fridge to grab the lunch I'd made the night before. "That's not the Molly you named me after."

When Mom was a kid she'd seen a musical called *The Unsinkable Molly Brown* and loved it. I threw my lunch into a paper bag and returned to the living room. "You told me I was named after Molly Brown, who started out dirt poor and became filthy rich. Who survived the sinking of the Titanic. Who had spunk and spirit. Who refused to give up, no matter what."

Mom looked at me disapprovingly. "Maybe I should have named you after the street vendor," she said and resumed playing.

I hurried toward the door and while I struggled to get my hand truck into the elevator, I could still hear Mom singing.

# Two

~~~~~~~~~

A *live, alive-o.*
The lyrics to "Molly Malone" floated around in my head as I walked toward Central Park. I laughed to myself.

Of course, technically speaking, I'm not a street vendor like dear old Molly Malone. Vendors need licenses, get hassled by police, and have to pay taxes. Me, I'm local color. So far, the police have ignored people like me who peddle handmade arts and crafts near the museum. New Yorkers agree we add to the tourists' enjoyment.

As I struggled to maneuver my hand truck across the curb on Broadway, some guy shouted at me from a car. "Hey Red, what're ya selling?" I ignored him. When I reached Central Park West, a construction worker up on a scaffolding whistled at my cutoff jeans. "Great shorts," he yelled down. "You want I should tear the rest off for ya?"

I looked up and shouted, "Haven't you got something better to do than stare at me? Is this why they pay you overtime?"

He laughed, scrawled something on a piece of paper, and watched it flutter to the ground. His phone number, I suppose. What a jerk!

As I crossed the street, I geared up for another workday. It's not all rosy, selling outdoors. The police don't hassle me, but passersby can drive me crazy. I hurried through the park, taking the tunnel route at Eighty-sixth Street to get there faster. On days when I have more time, I like to stroll a more scenic route. But I was already behind schedule and afraid my space would be taken.

I turned down Fifth Avenue anxious to reach Eighty-first Street, my heart literally pounding with anticipation.

I was in luck. My favorite spot—beneath the trees, slightly in from the curb, close to the cool spray of the fountain—was empty. Happily, I began to assemble my displays.

I can set up my merchandise in less than ten minutes. I unfold my collapsible card table, flip open my jewelry display boards, and prop up my matted collages. Then I'm in business.

There's an ongoing discussion among the vendors regarding the pros and cons of price tags. Some prefer to size up a customer, measure interest, then quote a price. But I think that's dishonest. All my items are prepriced. I never raise a price if I think a customer has lots of money—although sometimes I'll lower it if I feel a person appreciates my work but can't afford it.

There was still a light June breeze in the air, but I knew the day would be a scorcher by one o'clock. That's why it's important to find a shady space. Some vendors nearly pass out after sitting in the sun all day.

As I began unpacking, the old Argentinean man who sells leather belts was setting up his display, too. Lotte (who's slightly crazy) was unwrapping her handmade scarves and shawls, carefully laying them out on the sidewalk. Nobody ever buys anything from Lotte. She sprawls her scarves across the pavement, then curses anyone who accidentally steps on them. "Don't trash the merchandise!" she yells with a wild look in her eyes. Naturally, everyone backs off. My friend Leonard told me Lotte once designed accessories for a famous fashion house until the pressure gave her a nervous breakdown.

A young couple from the Southwest who sell turquoise and silver jewelry were setting up a few yards from me. As always, there were the usual licensed vendors peddling soft drinks, pretzels, ice cream, and hot dogs. And there are always a few artists of a slightly tackier variety who sell gross oil paintings—but to each his own.

I saw Rempha rushing down the street and waved to him. Actually, he hadn't transformed himself into Rempha yet; he was still Leonard. Leonard is a part-time actor, part-time waiter, part-time dancer who becomes Rempha the Mechanical Man, a part-time street performer. He smears himself with gold paint and puts on a gold suit, hat, shoes, and gloves. Then, accompanied by classical music from his portable tape deck, he slowly moves to the rhythms. When he initiated his act he called himself Leonard the Mechanical Man. He began getting bigger donations after he switched his sign. Leonard says the name Rempha comes from ancient Egyptian magic. Rempha was the genie of time—which I believe, because time stops when Leonard performs. He's like a perfectly synchronized machine, and I love watching him.

Leonard smiled and waved at me. "Hi!" he shouted, hurrying toward the museum's side entrance.

"Don't give them more than a penny," I shouted back.

That's our running gag. Leonard uses the museum's men's room to change into his outfit, so he has to pay admission. Their suggested donation is five dollars (which tourists always pay). Technically, you can pay what you wish, even a penny. So naturally that's what Leonard gives them. So do I. Of course, technically, Leonard isn't visiting the museum, only the men's room. But the principle is the same. Ideally, I think art in museums should be accessible to everyone without worrying about cost. If people have a need to see a Rembrandt or a Wyeth, they should be able to do it, even if they have no money. Besides, the Metropolitan is heavily funded, so they don't need my money. I save the maximum contribution for the Brooklyn Museum or others with smaller collections and fewer visitors.

Leonard keeps insisting that my philosophy is inconsistent—"Either you think art should be free or not"—but I guess I'm an inconsistent person.

Leonard bypassed the museum entrance to stop at my table. "Is that a new collage?" he asked, noticing my latest endeavor.

"Yes, I made it this morning."

He picked it up, obviously understanding its significance. "Does this mean you and that Isaac guy are finito?"

"That's right. Kaput."

A curious grin crossed Leonard's face then quickly turned into a more sympathetic expression. "Sorry. Want to talk about it?"

"I wouldn't bore you with the details."

"Go ahead, bore me."

I can't figure Leonard. He's only in his twenties, but I guess he doesn't have much of a social life because he's always interested in mine. "Let's say Isaac wasn't socially committed," I told him.

Leonard nodded knowingly. "A closet Yuppie, right? They're taking over everything."

For months, Leonard and I have been having lengthy philosophical discussions about what's wrong with the city, the country, the planet, and the universe. We've concluded that people committed exclusively to making money are responsible for the whole mess.

Leonard gestured toward the Greek hot dog vendor whose cart was parked at the south end of the museum. "Know what Theo bid for that spot this year? A hundred and ten thousand bucks, can you believe it?

14

He'll make a big profit, too. You should talk to him, Molly, he's one of 'em. He was telling me how important it is to have 'leverage in a high-volume spot.' He also quotes Nielsen reports on soda sales and reads *Forbes* magazine. The guy is definitely a closet Yuppie!" He put down my collage. "Sorry about you and what's-his-face."

"Forget it," I said. "What's new with you? Any good gigs coming up?"

"I've been offered a job at Disney World for the summer. They want me to be Mickey Mouse."

"You're kidding—how tacky! Are you going to do it?"

Leonard shrugged. "My friends say I should be grateful God dropped this gig in my lap—but I think God should've consulted me about it first. What if I don't want to be a rodent in Orlando?" He noticed a crowd forming by the steps of the Metropolitan. "I'd better change. I'll talk to you later."

When Leonard returned, he was totally transformed. He nodded as he passed me but didn't speak. Leonard rarely speaks once he's become Rempha. It's as if he takes on a whole new persona—one far greater than the sum of its parts. Sometimes that happens to me when I'm involved in my artwork. All the seemingly insignificant scraps and pieces I stick together suddenly combine to produce something much greater. With Leonard, it's this person he calls Rempha—whom I truly consider a wise being. It's a real joy to watch him, almost a religious experience. Rempha becomes so concentrated on what he does that the rest of the world falls away. He doesn't notice the heat, the noise, the kids tugging at him, the ghetto-blasters passing by. He is impervious to all of it—a majestic gold sentinel standing at the steps of Art. Only the tiny beads of perspiration popping out on his painted forehead reveal he is actually human.

As I stared at him posed in the golden glow of the late morning sunlight and watched his slow, subtle gestures, for a moment I felt transported. Then someone tapped me on the shoulder. "How much?" a man asked, pointing to one of my collages.

"Fifty dollars."

"I'll take it," he said. "I know just where to hang this. On my office wall when I get back to Albuquerque. It reminds me of the sun going down over Chaco Canyon."

With my collages the whole is definitely greater than the sum of its parts. Chaco Canyon! I didn't emphasize that I'd constructed it from orange-juice cartons, tea leaves, crushed pussy willows, sandbox sand, and burnt incense ash. Sometimes people feel art made from garbage has less value and therefore should cost less —which totally negates the value of the creative concept. I dusted my jewelry, adjusted my price labels, sat down on my folding chair, opened a book, and waited for more customers.

It *was* a slow day. By two o'clock I'd finished three chapters, and I'd only sold the collage and three small pins. The larger, trendier wearable art wasn't moving. I sized up the museum crowd. They looked too conservative for my stuff.

As I was unwrapping my egg-salad sandwich, Mrs.

Cavendish passed by. She's a housekeeper for a super-rich family on Fifth Avenue, and she always stops to chat with me. In fact, she often brings me lemonade on real hot days. "A sweet girl like you shouldn't have to do this," she tells me, refusing to believe I actually like what I do.

Mrs. Cavendish is a real old-fashioned mom type from England with a charming accent and an equally charming personality. I've often wondered if Mr. and Mrs. Worthington Spratt II (the rich people she works for) actually appreciate her. I hope so.

"What's new and different, Molly?" she asked, as usual.

"See for yourself," I said, as usual.

Mrs. Cavendish circled my jewelry display, carefully remarking on everything new. "Very interesting, yes, indeed."

I secretly suspect she considers my junk art actually just junk.

She cleared her throat. "I think I'll make a purchase today," she told me with proud resolve.

I was amazed. "C'mon, Mrs. C., this stuff isn't your style."

"No, your work is charming, Molly—very modern. As luck would have it, I need a snappy gift. Do you have any stickpins?"

I flipped the display board down to reveal the second layer. "They're awfully trendy."

"Perfect," she said. "Young people like the latest thing, don't they? I want a present for my boy, Ron. He's coming home from college."

I cringed as I watched her select my most far-out

design, made from twisted paper clips and computer parts. "Maybe you'd prefer something more conservative?"

"No, indeed," she insisted. "Ron is a trend setter. Once he wears this on campus all the other Harvard boys will want one, too."

I doubted it. In fact, I couldn't picture a Harvard guy wearing my junk-art jewelry. "Maybe he'd prefer brass," I suggested. "I've some great things I made from old furniture fittings—much more appropriate."

"You think so?"

"Sure," I told her, "but I didn't bring them today."

She looked disappointed. "What a shame. Ron is coming home tomorrow morning."

"I could drop it off tonight," I offered.

"That would be perfect, Molly, if you don't mind." She wrote down her address. "Ron has worked so hard this year, I'd like to give him a special gift. Made by someone special."

I was flattered. If Mrs. C.'s son was half as nice as she is, he must be an okay guy. And smart, too, to manage a scholarship to Harvard! I decided to give him the stickpin for free.

"But, Molly," she cautioned as if reading my mind, "no special price. I mean to pay you what the pin is worth. Before long you'll be going to college, too, and that takes lots of money."

"Not if I get into Cooper Union," I told her. "It's a free art college."

"Even so—well, you know." I could tell the money conversation was making Mrs. C. uncomfortable. She handed me a twenty-dollar bill. "Something nice. I leave it to you."

"I'll stop by after nine o'clock," I said, then waved as she walked on down the street.

I glanced at the address she had given me. It was one of the poshest buildings on Fifth Avenue—where Jackie O. and other millionaires rub noses, no doubt, and where the hottest topic of conversation in the elevator must be about whose maid is dating whose butler.

I smiled to myself, wondering what Mrs. Cavendish's M.R. must look like. Nothing like mine, I was willing to bet.

# Three

I t turned out to be a great day, after all.

By six o'clock I'd earned $160.00, much more than usual. Better still, a man from New Jersey bought my collage of Isaac. He explained he was a mathematician and he thought it represented Sir Isaac Newton—now that's something I wouldn't have thought of! With the collage gone, I felt like a new woman—free to resume my life sans Isaac—and free to see my kids.

The museum closes late on Fridays and Saturdays, so in the summer I often sell till 8:45 on Fridays. But on Saturday I like to leave at six so I can have more time with my kids.

I could hardly wait to see them.

I quickly packed my hand truck then waved good-bye to Rempha. I hurried toward Lexington Avenue and got on the downtown subway.

Going to the Prince George Hotel on East Twenty-eighth Street always fills me with a strange combination of feelings. I'm eager to see all my kids again, especially Mitchell, but it makes me sick to think of them living in such an awful place.

Midway out of the Thirty-fourth Street station, the train stalled. As passengers stared blankly at one another, waiting for it to start up again, I glanced out the subway window into the sooty darkness and thought back to the first time I met my kids.

Although it was only a few months earlier, it seemed much longer. I had been to Canal Street to pick up some cheap supplies, then I'd walked through Soho to drop off slides of my art at a gallery. Near Houston Street, I noticed a flattened packet from an empty crack vial lying in the street. Its colors looked interesting, so I picked it up. As I kept walking, I found more discarded crack containers, envelopes, vials, and caps all over the street. Then an idea hit me. I'd make them into a collage. Set against a map of the area, it would be a cartographic grid of downtown drug use.

I always get what I call "the buzz" whenever a great new art idea grabs me. It's sort of a high that comes when I know I've thought up a fabulous concept. I could see it completed: the multicolored caps and packets would form a tapestry of interconnected dots and patterns superimposed over the map. I got so excited I began combing the gutters for more discarded paraphernalia. People stared at me, but I didn't care; I'm used to it. I'm always scouting the streets for garbage. By the time I got to Twenty-eighth Street, I had a bagful of "junkie" junk.

Then I hit the mother lode!

Outside the Prince George Hotel, I saw dozens of empty crack vials and caps strewn across the sidewalk. As I started picking them up, a boy around nine years old pushed me aside. "Hands off that stuff," he shouted. "Get outta here, babe."

"Knock it off," I said. "What's it your business?" (I later learned that the neighborhood kids get paid by the drug dealers to recycle some of the discarded vials.)

"I mean it, man, get outta here," he shouted, then pushed me into the gutter.

My new box of pastel pencils fell to the sidewalk. Quick as a flash, the kid grabbed them then ran down the block and dashed into the hotel. Several mothers with little kids and babies were hanging around outside, but no one paid attention.

"That kid just stole my stuff!" I shouted.

I wasn't surprised they ignored me; they had their own problems. As I stared up at the entrance of the building with its torn awning and grimy brick façade, I knew it must be a welfare hotel. I hurried inside and glanced around for the boy. I saw dozens of kids of all sizes hanging out by the elevators, sitting on folding chairs, or crying in corners. As I walked around the dimly lit brown lobby, I sensed the hopelessness intermingled with the dust and dirt. The man at the desk looked dead-eyed and burned-out; someone who had seen too much and wanted to forget most of it.

I stared at the kids. Some were dirty; some looked hungry. I didn't see the boy who had stolen my pastels, so I left.

But I couldn't get the place out of my head. It reminded me of a Van Gogh painting called *The Night Cafe*. I think Van Gogh described it as a place where one can ruin oneself, go mad, or commit a crime. How could kids survive in such a hopeless atmosphere?

So the next day I went back. Only this time I brought a whole mess of art supplies with me. As fate would have it, the boy who'd stolen my pastels was standing at the entrance. He tried running when he saw me, but I grabbed him.

"Cool it. I've got something for you," I told him.

He looked scared. "What're you, some weird kinda junkie? What'd you go pickin' up that crap in the street for anyhow?"

"I'm an artist. Artists like weird crap. What'd you do with those pastels you ripped off from me yesterday?"

"I sold 'em," he said, trying to loosen my grip.

"How much did you get?" I asked, holding him tighter.

"Three bucks."

"You were robbed," I told him. "They're worth at least ten." I pulled him inside the lobby. "C'mon, I want to show you something."

By now he thought I was nuts. "I don't wanna see nothin', lady."

"Have you got a name?"

"Yeah, Antoine."

I found an empty corner of the lobby. "Okay, Antoine, shut up and sit down."

Antoine seemed a little scared of me, so he did it.

I would have bet anything short of murder was allowed in that lousy place, but I figured I should ask, anyway. I approached the desk clerk. "Is it okay if I draw some pictures for these kids? That's not against the rules, is it?"

The clerk droned out his reply as if it came from a tape inserted somewhere in his back. "No visitors upstairs. No cooking in the rooms, no refrigerators. Those are the rules."

"Thanks," I told him.

I sat down on the floor in the empty corner of the lobby. I dumped out some colored pencils and began to draw. A small dark-eyed girl with a runny nose was the first to come over. She stared down at my drawing. "What's that?" she asked brightly.

"It's a rabbit," I told her.

She wiped her nose on her sleeve. "The kind in Easter baskets?"

"No, this is a jackrabbit. They have much longer hind legs."

Antoine grew interested. "Who taught ya to draw so good?"

"Anyone can draw," I told him. "You just have to want to."

"*I* want to," the girl said.

I handed her some paper then spilled out a box of crayons. "Go ahead, pick some colors."

She sat down, spread open her legs, and pulled all

24

the crayons toward her. It was a gesture I remembered from my own childhood days in the sandbox, wanting all the sand. Her eyes darted across the colors, not knowing which ones to pick first. Then she grabbed four together, made a fist around them, and scrawled across the paper.

"That's great," I said, "you made a rainbow."

She smiled. "My name is Sonja."

"I'm Molly."

"I like you, Molly."

Antoine was feeling left out. "That's a sissy picture." He took some paper and began drawing what looked like a destroyer superhero. "I don't draw that dumb dude crap."

Sonja looked hurt. "Antoine had a breakdown," she said teasingly.

That sounded weird. Where did this little kid learn about stuff like that? I later learned most of the kids have a pile of psychiatric problems, diagnosed during random visits by therapists. But the therapists never get help for any of them, so they just learn to parrot the names of their disorders.

"Shut your face, shithead!" Antoine shouted.

"It's *true*," teased Sonja. "You couldn't stop crying—the lady said so."

Sonja and Antoine started fighting, which attracted other kids over to us. After a while there were seven of them wanting to draw pictures.

That's when I saw Mitchell.

Do you suppose there's one kid in the world for each of us who can turn our heart to mush? Mitchell

walked into the lobby with a sneer on his face, a chip
on his shoulder, and an angry attitude toward the
world. His sneakers had holes and his clothes and hair
were filthy. He reminded me of the boy Heathcliff in
*Wuthering Heights*. His big dark eyes seemed to soak in
everything like a sponge. And something about his
cynical face made him look much older.

I wanted him to join us. A look in his eyes told me
he wanted to, but he didn't. Instead, he stood in a
corner pretending he wasn't interested. Every time I
looked up, I caught him glancing over.

Sonja kept making colorful rainbows while Antoine
did his superhero thing. By now the other kids who
had joined us were all fighting over the supplies. I
dumped out several jars of poster color and some
brushes. "Look, you can paint, too," I told them.

Sonja was the first to try. The kids had never used
brushes before, so they made a big mess. I could tell
Mitchell was growing real interested, but I knew if I
invited him to join us he'd refuse.

Eventually he came over. "Whatchadoin?" he asked
coolly.

"We're painting pictures." I handed him some paper and a paintbrush. "Which colors would you like?"

He glanced at them all, carefully selecting three. I
think I knew right away he had talent. First, I noticed
the way he chose his colors, then the way he thought
before using each one. The minute his hands touched
the paper, I could see he was in another world. I recognized that look. Mitchell didn't make scribbles or
experiment like the other kids. He already had an image
in his mind, and he translated it to paper. He drew an

interesting abstract with several shapes interconnecting.

"That's very good," I told him.

He didn't respond, but I could see he was pleased I liked his work.

While the other kids began sharing with one another, making funny remarks about each other's drawings, Mitchell took his supplies to a separate corner and worked by himself.

Discreetly, I asked the other kids to tell me more about Mitchell. I learned he was twelve years old and he'd lived with his mother on the third floor ever since their tenement in Brooklyn burned down. That's all they knew.

That first day, I stayed at the Prince George Hotel for hours, supervising the kids' drawings and encouraging them to try new techniques. Mitchell never said another word. When I finally left, I promised to come back again. But it nearly broke my heart to leave those kids behind.

It always breaks my heart.

And even after all this time, Mitchell has barely spoken. But he waits for me. Sometimes he hangs out by the entrance anticipating my arrival. Once, when I was too sick to come, the other kids told me he waited for over an hour. Yet Mitchell never shares what he does. When he's finished he rolls up his artwork and goes upstairs. It makes me crazy, wondering what's going on inside that kid's head!

When the train finally pulled into the Twenty-eighth Street station, I pushed off my hand truck. As always,

I made a quick inspection of the side street, looking for promising garbage. The area around the Prince George is like lots of other sections in Manhattan where various neighborhoods converge. A few blocks one way there are high-rise office buildings; a few blocks another way are fancy Park Avenue apartments; a few blocks down-town there's a bustling shopping district. So there are often interesting things piled beside the garbage cans. I found a cardboard box filled with discarded computer chips, put a few in my bag, and then walked to the hotel.

Halfway down the block I stopped to exchange a high-five with Antoine.

"Hi teach, you back again?" (He asks me that every time.)

"You bet. Are you ready for me?"

"Yo, gotta grab a soda first, catch you up."

I waved toward the grimy hotel windows, where several of my kids were looking out, and gestured for them to come downstairs. Mitchell was peeking out of the entranceway. When he noticed me coming, he ducked back into the lobby.

A real cool customer, that one!

Sonja hurried over and hugged me. "What did you bring? Something pretty?"

"Something interesting," I told her.

She looked sulky. "I like pretty."

Sonja loves the look and feel of art supplies and uses them all. But she rarely experiments; she usually makes rainbows. Darryl tries everything, too, but he usually makes a big mess in the process. Each kid has different habits and each draws different things, but they all look forward to new materials. I unloaded my art bag and took out a ten-pound box of clay. I opened it and dumped it onto a wooden board just as Antoine was returning.

He started to laugh. "Hey man, that stuff looks like dog shit."

"Yeah—it's not pretty," Sonja complained.

"But you can make pretty things with it," I explained. "This is self-hardening clay, so you don't need a kiln."

"What's a kiln?" asked Darryl.

"An oven. Some clay needs to bake in an oven to get hard, but this kind hardens as it dries. C'mon, let's all make something. The next time I come I'll bring special paints so you can glaze your work."

"What's glaze?" asked Sonja.

"Pretty colors," I told her.

As I pulled off chunks of clay and handed them out, I noticed one of my kids was missing. "Where's Carmen?"

"She can't come down," said Darryl. "She cut open her mouth real bad."

"How'd that happen?" I asked.

"She fell outa bed," said Darryl.

Antoine shoved him. "That's 'cause Carmen ain't got no *real* bed, man, just a cot."

"Did she see a doctor?" I asked.

Sonja stared at me as if I were crazy. "Ain't no doctors here," she told me.

Carmen is the youngest of my kids, only five. I

glanced over and saw Mitchell staring at me (accusingly, I thought). When I gave him some clay he retreated into his usual corner. I began to show the other kids how to mold and shape the clay with the wooden sculpting tools I'd brought, but, as usual, Mitchell didn't need instruction. He dug away the sides of clay, instinctively knowing how to bring what he envisioned to life. Before long, he'd created a primitive Mexican-type mask, and he was busy forming eyeholes.

"Someday you kids will put together great portfolios," I told them.

"What's a portfolio?" asked Monty.

"It's a book of all your artwork," I explained. "You'll need it if you want to get into the High School of the Arts."

"Is that where you go?" asked Sonja.

"You bet. I learn lots of things about art there, and I get to draw and paint every day." I glanced at Mitchell to make sure all this was registering. "It's a great high school for kids who love art."

"Do you have to be rich to go there?" asked Sonja.

"No, it's free," I told her. "All the supplies are free, too. So you can paint, draw, sculpt, and do collages."

"What's collages?" asked Monty.

I removed one from my hand truck to show them. "But that's the subject for another art lesson," I told him. "How are you doing with the clay?"

I glanced at everyone's work. Monty was building a pyramid, Darryl was sculpting a head, and Sonja was rolling out strips of clay (for rainbows, of course). Mitchell's mask had acquired lots more character and depth.

30

"That's very good," I told him. "There's a mask like that in the Museum of Natural History. I could take you there and show it to you someday. Would you like that?"

He didn't answer.

"Would any of you guys like to come to the museum with me?" I asked. No one answered, which didn't surprise me. I'm always offering to take them to various museums, but they never accept, and I've a feeling they're all afraid to explore unknown places. But I keep trying.

When Mitchell finished, he took his mask and went upstairs without saying a word to me.

Yep, he's a mighty cool customer, that Mitchell is!

# Four

When I got home, Mom was napping on the sofa with a damp washcloth covering her eyes. One of her students must've acted up and given her a headache.

I went into the M.R. and checked through my inventory for a pin for Mrs. C.'s son. At a flea market, I'd found a great batch of Victorian brass furniture fittings, corroded but beautiful. Because they were green and cruddy, the vendor gave me a good deal. I'd polished them up and made them into stickpins. I selected my favorite—a pig with a macho stride and a hobo satchel slung across his shoulder. He looked like a real cocky dude, ready to hit you in the chops. He wasn't at all like my favorite pig, Wilbur in *Charlotte's Web*, but I liked his self-assured attitude. If Mrs. C.'s son had a sense of humor, he'd like him, too. I wrapped the pin in tissue paper.

As I hurried to the front door, Mom stirred. "Is that you, Molly?" she asked, peeking over the cloth.

"In the flesh—but I've got to go."

"Bring back Chinese," she pleaded, "I'm starving," then covered up her eyes again.

It was already after nine o'clock when I took the crosstown bus to Fifth Avenue. Mrs. Cavendish's building was definitely upper-upper, but it wasn't one of those new glass and flash deals. This was the old-money type that will still be standing after a nuclear disaster. The mosaic tiles in the lobby looked priceless, as if Leonardo had set them there himself. And the entrance was huge.

"You need a map to find your way around in here," I joked.

The doorman wasn't amused. He asked where I was going, then rang up to check me out. "Take the elevator to A Wing, eighteenth floor," he told me, with no emotion penetrating his stony expression.

I noticed his uniform was color-coordinated with the black, gray, and tan mosaic tiles on the floor. And his brass buttons accented the brass lighting fixtures. No accident, I'm sure. These guys get their duds custom-made. After all, they're the building owners' reps out there on the street. "Nice fabric," I commented. "Does the tailor come around in person to measure you?"

He ignored my question. "Go to A Wing," he repeated. Maybe he assumed I'd be impressed by his haughtiness, but I wasn't.

The elevator man, wearing an equally nifty uniform, took me to the eighteenth floor. This opened onto another lobby where a bronze urn filled with fresh flowers rested on a gilt table. The walls were covered with lemon-yellow moiré silk and the thick mahogany door had a large brass knocker. But I didn't need to knock. Mrs. C. greeted me as the elevator opened.

"Molly, I've caused you such bother," she apologized. "It's Saturday night. You're probably missing a date."

That comment brought back a momentary twinge of longing for Isaac. I wondered what he was doing, but the feeling quickly passed. "No, I'm in between dates," I replied.

The phone rang and Mrs. C. hurried inside to answer it, so I followed. "Spratt residence," she announced as I glanced around. The place looked like it was waiting for its *Architectural Digest* layout. It was over-draped, over-lacquered, over-mirrored, and over-done. It had probably just been redesigned by the hottest decorator in town. I felt claustrophobic in there.

As Mrs. Cavendish jotted down a message, she gestured for me to have a seat. The white suede sofa looked too imposing. I kept standing.

"What a hectic day," she said. "The Spratts are returning from Europe this week."

The apartment was so fancy, it made me feel uncomfortable. "Yes, I've had a busy day, too, but I wanted to bring you this pin," I told her.

Another phone rang somewhere else in the apartment, and Mrs. C. went to answer it. I glanced at the panoramic view of Central Park through the picture windows. It wasn't high enough for people below to look like the proverbial ants, but they were already beginning to take on an unreal quality. I thought of the dingy lobby of the Prince George Hotel where I'd been only an hour earlier, and I started feeling weird. Suddenly I had to get out of there.

Mrs. Cavendish returned.

"I've got to go," I told her.

"Wait," she said, "I have something for you. It was being thrown out and I thought of you. That sounds dreadful, doesn't it? But I know you use—well—unusual things in your artwork."

I was getting curious. "What is it?"

"See for yourself." Mrs. C. led me through the dining room past the bedrooms and the study, toward a room adjoining the kitchen. At first I thought it must be her personal M.R., but I was wrong. As she opened the door I saw nothing inside but an ironing board, some boxes, and a basket stacked with shirts.

"What's this, the ironing room?" I joked.

"That's right. Mr. Spratt prefers his shirts done at home." She pointed to the box beside the ironing board. "It's over there. When the decorator redid the bedrooms, he found it in a closet."

I *knew* there'd been a decorator lurking around there lately.

"Mrs. Spratt insisted it was useless old clutter, but I thought it might be just the thing for you, Molly."

Inside the box were dozens of old postcards sent from all corners of the world. Lots of them dated back to the turn of the century. There were photos of Big Ben, the pyramids, and lots of posh hotels that probably don't exist anymore. The Spratts' ancestors and their rich friends got around. I read through some of the cards written back in the old days of fountain pens and fine penmanship. "What a gold mine! This stuff is perfect for my collages." I wasn't sure what kind of social statement I could make with them, but I'm always interested in tracking the roots of things visually. I might make them part of an assemblage depicting immigrant travel versus first-class passage in different decades.

Mrs. Cavendish looked pleased. "I knew you would like them. I think old things have character, don't you?"

"And spirit," I added. "Sometimes I can feel people's vibes hanging around old things."

"Like ghosts?" she asked.

"Sort of—but good ghosts, if you know what I mean."

"Well, as long as it comes in handy," she said.

"This stuff is priceless," I told her, closing the box. Then I gave her the pin.

She unwrapped the tissue paper and smiled. "It's very humorous. Ron will love it. I'm sure he'll put it on his jacket right away."

"That's good," I said, returning the twenty dollars she'd given me.

"No, Molly, I told you I wouldn't accept a gift."

"It's not a gift; it's barter. This box of cards would cost me much more at a flea market, so it's a fair exchange."

36

"I don't agree," she said sternly. "You deserve payment for your labor."

"Forget it, Mrs. C. Remember what Willy Shakespeare wrote—he who steals my purse steals trash—and in my case, trash is more valuable than my purse."

"No, this isn't right," she protested.

I lifted the card box. "Don't worry about it."

"Won't you at least stay for tea?" she asked, following me to the door.

"Another time," I said, pressing the elevator button. "I hope your son enjoys the pin. Tell him to stop by tomorrow and let me know. I'll be selling in my usual spot outside the museum."

Mrs. C. opened her mouth as if to say something, but just then the elevator doors opened. I glanced at the liveried elevator operator. His gold-braided hat, huge epaulets, shiny brass buttons, and the razor-sharp pleat in his trousers made him look like he was ready for battle. "Straight to the lobby, General," I ordered, "and take no prisoners on the way."

Outside, the doorman looked just as snooty as before. "You're doing a great job out here," I teased. "Yep, the owners must be proud!"

Back on the West Side, I picked up some Chinese food, then headed home. When I arrived back in my own lobby, I noticed Mom hadn't checked the mail. As I removed it from our mailbox, Mrs. Prentice was putting the key into hers. She threw me a nasty glance, and I wondered what was up. Mrs. Prentice's daughter, Tiffany, is one of Mom's piano students.

"I've been calling your house all day, but no one ever answered," she told me.

"Mom keeps the phone unplugged during classes," I explained.

"Oh?" she said with annoyance. "You should get an answering machine. It's very inconvenient to keep calling."

I've never liked Mrs. Prentice. She always has an attitude. "Can I take the message?" I offered.

She cleared her throat. "Yes, tell your mother I'm very upset. After all, I'm paying her good money to teach Tiffany to play Mozart. This week she came home after her lesson and played me something she said was called 'I Ain't Down Yet.' It was certainly not Mozart." Mrs. Prentice glared at me a moment for dramatic punctuation. I tried to stifle a grin.

"That's a song from a Broadway musical called *The Unsinkable Molly Brown*," I explained.

Obviously, she didn't appreciate my amusement. Her tone grew sharper. "Normally, I'm not one to complain," she assured me. "After all, I hired your mother knowing she had no classical training in piano. And no teaching experience, either. But I hired her nonetheless."

Before Mom taught piano, she was a cocktail pianist. Okay, so maybe sometimes she thinks she's still in hotels, wearing her rhinestone pumps with a brandy snifter stuffed with dollar bills on the piano. But so what? Mom gets along great with her students, and all the kids think she's terrific. Maybe it's because she does bang out "I Ain't Down Yet" once in a while. That used

38

to be her theme song. And if Mrs. Prentice prefers a conservatory-trained teacher, let her get one. I'd like to see her find one for the rates Mom charges!

Mrs. Prentice leafed through her junk mail. "Will you remember to deliver that message, Molly?" she asked pointedly.

"Sure I will," I said lightly. "No more frivolous musical numbers. Right?"

She nodded and walked toward the elevator. "Are you coming up?"

"No," I said evasively, perusing the mail, "not yet."

When the elevator returned to the lobby, I got in. As I rode up alone, a wistful childhood memory floated through my mind . . . The sound of Mom's high heels as she tiptoed into my room after I'd gone to bed . . . Mom gently humming her theme song as she tucked me in . . . Mom making a tiny sign of the cross on my forehead in the darkness and whispering in my ear, "Pray I get lots of big, juicy tips tonight, Molly. Pray we get rich!"

# Five

The next morning I was in a rotten mood. It looked like it would be a beastly hot day and the thought of selling on the street in the heat put me off.

I couldn't get the lead out. As I dragged my cart through the park like a slug, I realized it was because I hadn't really slept the night before. Not a good sleep, only crummy dreams I'd forgotten.

I'd also forgotten to give Mom the message from Mrs. Prentice. I'd definitely started off the day with two left feet, and the way it was going, I was afraid all the shady selling spots would already be taken. There I'd be in my cutoff jeans and halter top, certain to fry to a crisp in the sunshine. Luckily, I arrived moments before Lotte staked her claim to the last shady spot. I snuck in real fast before she could and quickly began setting up.

By twelve o'clock I had sold three pairs of earrings and two drawings. Not bad. I reached for my sandwich and realized I'd forgotten to pack it. Just when I was beginning to hear my stomach grumble from hunger, something happened to take my mind off food.

Mrs. Cavendish's son stopped by.

He was wearing my pig stickpin in his lapel. That's how I recognized him. I also noticed he was tall and handsome. Not handsome enough for him to be carried away over it, but sufficient for all practical purposes.

As he stood over my table, his wavy light brown hair kept slipping down over his forehead. "I like the stickpin," he told me. "Thanks. I'm Cameron—uh, Ron."

"Nice to meet you. Glad you like it. I wasn't sure. After all—a pig . . ."

"No, he's great, really—radiant and humble."

I could hardly believe my ears. "No, he isn't."

Ron nodded. "You're right—he's not humble. I was actually referring to—"

"I know. Wilbur."

"That's right," he said, smiling. "*Charlotte's Web* was my favorite book as a kid."

"Mine, too," I told him. My heart started pounding. Shorthand. It had been my dream to someday meet a guy I could talk with in shorthand. I'd thought that only happened after years of being together. I had to test it out. "Since we're on the subject of E. B. White, do you think Stuart Little ever found Margalo?"

Ron shrugged. "I'm not sure. I still have sleepless nights wondering about it."

"So do I!" We both smiled.

Ron glanced at my artwork. "Your collages are great. Do you have a gallery?"

"Is there a Santa Claus?"

"I guess I don't know that much about it."

"Yeah, well, unless you can walk on water, it's hard. But I keep making the rounds of galleries, trying to get appointments."

"Just like an actor, I guess. Always auditioning?"

I shrugged. "Maybe. Only I think breaking into the art field is even harder than breaking into show business. Gallery directors usually don't see people, only slides."

"It's that hard?"

"It's not easy. So I guess I'll be selling on the street until fame catches up with me."

"It must get awfully cold out here in winter."

"It does. That's when I switch to the Seventy-seventh Street flea market on Sundays. It's indoors."

"I see," said Ron. He examined my collages a long time.

"Is there one you like in particular?"

"I like them all," he told me, "but I can't buy any. I'm nearly busted."

I was pleased he seemed so interested. "Relax, it doesn't cost anything to look."

After a while Ron glanced up from the artwork and started to examine *me*. "I was wondering, can you get away from here?"

I ran my hand over my display table. "Are you proposing to take me away from all this?" I joked.

"Just for a while," he said. "I thought we could have coffee or something. Maybe we could discuss some more subtleties of E. B. White. Have you ever read his letters?"

"Sure I have," I told him, "but I can't get away. I have no one to watch my things."

"Oh," he said disappointedly. "I guess I thought you took a lunch break."

"I usually do, but lunch is a sandwich right here. Only today I forgot to bring my sandwich."

He shrugged. "I understand. Maybe some other time."

I couldn't let my golden opportunity pass.

"Maybe I could check my stuff in the museum," I suggested. "Would you like to have a cup of coffee in there?"

"Sure," he said, awkwardly looking through his wallet. "I've enough for coffee but not two admission fees, and we might want to look at some paintings afterward."

"Don't worry about the admission fee," I reassured him. "I never pay more than a penny." I took two cents from my pocket. "See, we're rich."

Ron smiled with relief. "Can I help you pack up your things?"

"No thanks, I'm a whiz at it." Within five minutes everything was set neatly on my hand truck. "Ready to roll." I pushed the truck into the side entrance of the Metropolitan and wheeled it over to the coat check counter.

The attendant stared down at it. "I can't check that thing," he said.

"Why not?" I asked. "You've got strollers checked over there, right? I see a suitcase, too. How come you can't check this?"

"Those are allowed," he argued. "Checking this big thing is against the rules."

"Oh really?" I asked, glancing around. "Where's that written? Show me the sign that says no hand trucks. Huh?"

The attendant rolled his eyes and grunted. Then he dragged my hand truck into a corner, slapped a ticket on it, and gave me the corresponding ticket.

"Thank you," I told him.

As we left the coat check, Ron glanced sideways at me. I couldn't tell if it was out of approval or amusement. Then when we approached the cashier, he said, "Hold it, I've never paid a penny before."

"Are you embarrassed?" I asked.

"I guess so," he admitted.

"Then I'll pay for both of us," I said. I plunked two pennies onto the counter. "That's for two, please."

The cashier seemed startled. "Two?"

"That's right," I said. *Two.*"

She sneered but rang up the two cents and handed me two admission buttons. "Sometimes they can get real huffy," I said, handing Ron his button. "You'd think they were earning a commission." As we walked toward the restaurant, I noticed a long line of people waiting outside. "It'll take forever before we're seated," I observed.

"Would you rather skip the coffee and just look at paintings?" Ron suggested.

"Sure. I know where all the best things are."

"So do I."

"I figured you would," I told him.

"How come?" he asked.

"Because you live so close. I bet you've come here hundreds of times."

"Often enough," Ron admitted. "When I was a kid, sometimes I'd pretend I lived here."

"No kidding?" I asked excitedly. "So did I. I used to pretend I slept in—"

"The big bed off the Medieval Hall?" he asked.

"That's right," I said, and we both laughed. "I played another game, too. I'd pretend everything here was for sale but I only had enough money to buy one painting. Then I'd spend hours wandering around deciding which one I wanted. Did you ever play that?"

"Never," Ron said.

"Would you like to play it now?" I asked. "You go first."

"Hold it, give me a chance to think. If I'm spending money, I need to make the right choice. First, I have to see what's available."

"Relax, it's only pretend money. Don't waffle. You know the inventory here as well as I do."

"That's true, but I've the feeling you're using this game as some sort of psychological test," he said suspiciously. "Sizing me up."

"So what if I am?"

"Okay, I'll play," he conceded, "but *you* go first."

"Sure, follow me." As we took the elevator to the second floor, two guards stopped us to make sure we were wearing our admission buttons. (I swear, they're absolutely obsessed about it.) Before we reached the Impressionist area, we entered a corner room. "That's the one I'd buy." I pointed to the portrait of *Mademoiselle Charlotte du Val d'Ognes*. It's attributed to an unknown French painter now, but it was probably done in 1800 by Constance Marie Charpentier.

It's a bold, simple painting of a young girl in a white dress seated sketching in her barren studio. Light from the cracked window beside her falls across her drawing. Through the window, a romantic couple is walking along a parapet in the distance. The world inside the artist's studio seems strangely removed from the world outdoors. She stares at the viewer, who is presumably the subject of her sketch.

"Why this one?" Ron asked.

"Lots of reasons," I explained. "The girl's face is timeless, the background is understated, and the color scheme is subtle. It combines the serenity of Vermeer and the tones of Rembrandt. And it also proves my point about the disgustingly sexist nature of art. When the Met acquired this painting in 1922, everyone thought it had been done by Jacques-Louis David, so art critics labeled it a masterpiece. Later when they thought it was painted by a woman, they suddenly changed their minds. Know why? Because women were considered incapable of artistic genius." I stared at the painting admiringly. "But Charlotte keeps sitting there, staring out to tell us otherwise. And now they're not sure who did it. But I'm sure it was a woman. And she and Charlotte will have the last laugh."

Ron nodded. "So you think she's a rallying point for female artists?"

"You bet. She's a great symbol. Through Charlotte, Constance Charpentier or a woman even more forgotten and obscure gives encouragement to all female artists who feel isolated."

"Maybe," Ron agreed. "I've always admired it, but it's too premeditated. Studio stuff. I'd pick something with more passion. More guts."

"Such as?"

Ron led me through the large room of Impressionist paintings until we reached the wall where some Van Goghs were hanging.

"So you like Vincent, eh? Which one is your favorite?"

Ron pointed to the painting *Irises*. "It's got everything," he said excitedly. "Color, style, movement. Those are real flowers, Molly. They look like they've just been cut. Can't you almost smell them?"

"I don't think irises have much of a smell," I noted.

"Everything Van Gogh did is still bursting with life. Read what he said about this painting." Ron gestured to the plaque beside it. "In a letter to his brother Theo, Van Gogh explained that with *Irises*, he was trying to express the love of two lovers by a wedding of complementary colors, their mingling and their opposition and the mysterious vibration of kindred tones. Isn't that beautiful?"

"Yes, it's very romantic," I agreed. "Van Gogh was great. But this painting depresses me."

"Why?"

"When I look at it, I think of his other painting of irises. The one that sold for over fifty million at Sotheby's. What a disgusting amount."

"But it's not the highest price for a Van Gogh," Ron said. "His *Portrait of Dr. Gachet* sold for eighty-two and a half million at Christie's."

"I know that," I told him. "That's what's so disgusting. The Gachet portrait sold for an inflated price because *Irises* sold for so much. And Sotheby's floated a loan to the buyer of *Irises*. Even though they foreclosed on the deal later, the damage to the art market had already been done."

"What Sotheby's did wasn't illegal," Ron argued.

"Who cares? It's unfair," I told him. "Keeping prices lower makes it possible for little museums with growing collections to remain in the art market. Otherwise, when priceless artworks come up for sale, small museums are always outbid. Only mega-museums are in the running. Or what's worse, private fat cats wind up with all the world's masterpieces."

"Are we discussing the art market or the commodities market?" Ron asked. "Or is there a difference?"

"There should be. Businessmen have no business in the art world."

Ron laughed. "I think that's a contradiction in terms. Anyway, you can't keep business out."

"Well, it makes me sick, especially when I think of the tragic life Van Gogh lived."

48

"Right," Ron teased, "cutting off part of his ear and all."

"I'm serious. It's obscene when you realize Van Gogh only sold one painting in his entire lifetime for the equivalent of about eighty dollars. And now that he's dead he's worth over eighty million."

"You think he's rolling over in his grave?"

"Sure I do. Don't you?"

"No," Ron said, "I think he's laughing. I bet he's happy he's finally getting recognition, especially since he couldn't give away his work when he was alive. I'm sure he'd see the irony of it. But you're right about his tragic life. I wouldn't trade with him, not for all his genius. And his tragic death, too. I think if I were an artist, I'd prefer to die the way Thomas Hart Benton did."

"How did he die?" I asked.

"He went in to dinner one evening after finishing a mural. Later, when he returned to his studio to sign it, he just dropped dead. Benton was in his eighties. Don't you think that's a perfect death for an artist?"

"Symmetrical, maybe, but boring. I'd prefer to be Van Gogh, even with all his pain."

"No pain, no gain?"

"Maybe. After all, Benton painted the same stuff all his life, didn't he? He never changed. I'll bet his last mural looked just like stuff he'd painted thirty years earlier. There's no point to a long life if you don't grow and change. Van Gogh will be around centuries after Benton is forgotten."

"Maybe so," Ron conceded. "Well, we've bought

our paintings, so what have we learned about each other? That you're a feminist. And that I'm more romantic? And more commercially practical." He glanced at me with his sparkling gray eyes. He looked so cute, like a little kid. "Do you have time to play another game with me?"

"Sure. My own crass commercialism can wait a little longer. What'll we play next? You pick it this time."

"All right," he said enthusiastically. "Let's see— okay, if you could inhabit a work of art, which one would you choose?"

"You mean go into it? Hey, I need to think about that. The possibilities are endless."

"No hedging, just pick one," he insisted.

I didn't have to go far. In an adjoining room of the Impressionist wing, there are two paintings practically facing one another, and they're both life-size canvases. One is *Joan of Arc* by Jules Bastien-Lepage. It's a marvelous painting of Joan as a young peasant girl, standing in the woods. There are two apparitions behind her in the trees; one of her as a maiden, the other dressed in battle armor. Joan stands toward the right of the canvas, one arm extended outward. She's looking at something the viewer can't see.

"Isn't that a great artistic concept?" I asked. "As viewers, we see something Joan can't, and she sees something we don't. I often wonder what she's looking at. I'll never know unless I get into the painting. I'll bet it's a heavenly vision. Maybe if I saw it, I'd know the meaning of life."

"So you'd like to know officially if there's a God? Ron asked. "You don't ask much, do you?"

"Wait, I haven't decided yet." I turned around to look at *The Horse Fair* by Rosa Bonheur. It's a majestic painting of men bringing huge draft horses to market. Alive with movement, the horses rear and prance as the men, looking dwarfed beside them, attempt to keep them in control. Bonheur's handling of color is brilliant. Although the painting is filled with light, the sky is actually cloudy.

"Another female artist," Ron noted. "Are you sure you're not prejudiced?"

"No, Rosa Bonheur was marvelous. Whenever I look at this painting, I can smell the air and hear the horses' hooves. I'm halfway into it already, so I might as well go all the way. Do you know what some people called Bonheur? A horse painter. Isn't that ridiculous? Her paintings encompass all of life. They're vibrant with energy and wisdom. Still, stupid people try to minimize her contribution because she's a woman."

"Hold it," Ron argued. "There are lots of famous women artists who get recognition."

"Don't mention Georgia O'Keeffe, she's the exception."

"Louise Nevelson?"

"Two exceptions."

"Mary Cassatt? Berthe Morisot? Alice Neel?"

"*All* exceptions," I insisted. "Throughout history, women artists have been passed over or trivialized, and nothing has changed. That's why I plan to join the Guerrilla Girls."

"Jungle warfare?"

"The Guerrilla Girls is an organization of female artists dedicated to getting more museum space for

51

women. They're working hard debunking the myth that genius in art is exclusively male. Less than five percent of artists in museums are women but eighty-five percent of the nudes are female. It's too bad they have to wear gorilla masks to get their message across, but it's their way of lashing out against sexism.''

Ron grinned, then stared down at my feet.

"What are you doing?" I asked.

"Looking for your soapbox."

"Never mind the wisecracks. It's your turn. Now, which painting would you inhabit?"

"It's not a painting; it's an environment."

"Lead on," I told him.

I followed Ron downstairs, across the Great Hall and into the American Wing. In a corner off the Garden Court there's a reconstructed room designed by Frank Lloyd Wright. Like everything Wright designed, this room is simple and understated, right down to the furniture and the stained glass windows.

"I'm crazy about this room," Ron said. "I could move in this minute."

I was surprised Ron would select such simplicity after growing up in the Spratt apartment surrounded by gilt and rococo. "This doesn't look much like the decor you live with," I noted. "I guess that place isn't your taste or your mother's."

"My mother didn't decorate the apartment," Ron said.

"I know. I guess she can't be held responsible for the taste of the Spratts. What's it like living with super-rich people like that?"

Ron stared at me, and I wondered if I'd offended him.

"What do you mean, what's it like?" he asked defensively. "People are people. Besides," he added, obviously wanting to change the subject, "that apartment doesn't reflect my taste. Wright is my taste. Have you ever visited Fallingwater?"

"Is that the house he built in Pennsylvania on top of a waterfall?"

"That's right."

"No, I've never been there."

"You've got to go," he said excitedly. "Any other architect would have built the house facing the falls. But Wright built above them so the house would literally become part of its natural setting. Everything about it is brilliant—inside and out. It's made of local stone and the woods can be seen from all the windows. This makes the house and its surroundings become one. And Wright also designed all the furniture. It's one of the two architectural wonders of the modern world: Chartres Cathedral and Fallingwater. And Wright built it despite the fact many engineers told him it was impossible. Lots of them swore it would fall down. But it will probably last as long as the pyramids. That's architectural genius!"

The enthusiasm in Ron's tone reminded me of how I feel when I'm really into my work. "Are you studying to be an architect?" I asked.

"No. Why? Did that sound like a lesson from Architecture 101?"

"Not unless I sound like Feminism 101. I guess we both have strong opinions."

"I guess we do," Ron agreed. He glanced at his watch. "Hey, I've got to run. I can't believe we've been in here so long."

"Neither can I," I said.

"This has been fun," he said. "Looking at art with you has been very . . ."

"Stimulating?"

He laughed. "Exactly."

"Yeah, well, I'm the stimulating type."

Ron stared at me. "I'm beginning to think so." I could tell he didn't want our time together to end. "If I weren't so broke I'd ask you out to dinner or the theater or something. I hear there's a good Ira Levin play about ghosts in a synagogue."

"I love Levin," I told him. "That sounds like fun."

"Yes it does, but . . ."

"Listen, that show is playing off Broadway, so we can get in free."

"How?"

"Trust me. What night is good for you?"

"Any night, I guess. How about you?"

I could hardly wait. "How about this Tuesday?"

"Fine. It's a date. But how're we—"

"Don't worry about it," I assured him. "Meet me outside the theater at seven. And wear a tie and a white shirt, okay?"

Ron was enjoying the mystery. "Is this another game? No, never mind, don't tell me. I'll be there."

We walked toward the side exit, where I picked up my hand truck. As we left the cool of the museum, a blast of warm afternoon air smacked me in the face.

For a second it felt really weird, like I'd switched from one reality into another.

"I've had a great time," Ron said. "See you on Tuesday, Molly."

I felt a little shiver run through me when I heard Ron say my name. He waved and hurried down the street. I stared after him a minute, sighing dreamily. Then I psyched myself up for going back to work. Luckily, no one had taken over my space.

As I reassembled my display, Rempha came over. "What happened to you?" Leonard asked, dabbing his gold-painted face with a tissue. "I thought you'd been kidnapped."

I looked up in surprise. "How come you're talking? You don't usually break out of character."

"And you don't usually leave your spot. I guess we both made an exception today. Where'd you go?"

"Into the museum. To look at art."

"How come?" he asked glibly. "Have you been taking that night course?"

I didn't know what he meant. "What course?"

"How to Meet Your Mate in the Great Museums. It's a course at The Learning Annex," he explained. "It teaches people how to hit on one another while pretending to appreciate art."

"Very funny."

"No, it's for real," he assured me. "So who's the guy?"

I didn't think it was his business. "What guy?"

"The Yup in the Gucci loafers."

"Ron? He's not a Yup. He's Mrs. Cavendish's son. He has a scholarship to Harvard."

"That's good, because his shoes cost a hundred bucks apiece."

Ron *had* looked well dressed, but very casual. "No way. He was wearing Woody Allen–type stuff."

"I know," said Leonard smugly. "Woody's knock-around wardrobe is designed by Ralph Lauren. That guy's a Yup, Molly."

I don't like guys who are into clothes. It's such a superficial thing and shows a basic lack of character. My dad was like that. As long as he had a carnation in his lapel and a shine on his shoes he thought he could fool the world. But he only fooled Mom.

"His jacket was Perry Ellis," Leonard continued. "At least three hundred at discount."

"How do you know?"

"My family is in the rag business. Trust me, that guy had a fortune on his back."

Was Leonard right? Was that why Ron was busted? Was a superficial clotheshorse lurking behind Ron's charming smile? How could anyone I had shared such a great discussion with be superficial?

Leonard stared at me stoically. Only it wasn't Leonard staring, it was Rempha, the majestic wise man who had come to predict the tragic future awaiting Molly Malone . . . wherein the fearful truth unfolds: Molly shall fall for a superficial hunk as her mother hath done before her.

At least Isaac wasn't a clotheshorse. Okay, so he didn't care much about social issues, but he didn't care much about his wardrobe, either.

I stared back at Leonard. "So you're taking an awfully long break. You've always said you'd rather die or starve than step out of character."

"And how come you're getting so touchy?"

"Am I?" Just then someone passed my spot and asked about my jewelry. "Excuse me," I said coolly, "I've got a customer."

Leonard shrugged and walked away.

Had I been touchy?

I wondered.

# Six

As I dragged my hand truck through Central Park, I reviewed the conversation I'd had with Ron. It left a warm glow.

When I arrived home, Mom was on the telephone. It didn't take long to realize she was talking to Mrs. Prentice, who was obviously chewing her out regarding Tiffany's musical education.

"I'm sorry you feel that way," Mom said, trying to adopt a haughty tone. "There's no point in arguing about it. I won't discuss musical appreciation with amateurs. Besides, who's to say Mozart is so terrific? In another hundred years, he may be forgotten. Did you ever think of that?" Mom slammed down the phone.

"I'm sorry," I told her. "I forgot to mention that Mrs. Prentice complained."

Mom sighed. "If it wasn't about this, it would've been something else. That woman is so sour. Let her cancel Tiffany's lessons, who cares." Mom walked to the hall mirror to fluff up her hair and check for lines around her eyes. She slapped herself under the chin, then looked approving. "I, as they say, have other fish to fry."

"What kind of fish?" I asked uneasily.

Mom smiled and pulled me toward her. "Remember that rhyme you loved when you were little?" She grabbed my hand and made a circular motion in my palm as she recited it: "We'll have a little fishy in a little dishy when our boat comes in."

"I remember it," I said. When Dad was alive, Mom always sang it to me at night before she went off to work. So that was it. I'd seen the signs before. Mom was toying with the idea of going back into show business. "Don't worry about losing Tiffany," I said. "You can get ten more students like her any day."

"I don't want ten more," Mom protested. "Tiffany Prentice is a little old lady. I always feel she's scrutinizing me. Frankly, I thought teaching her a few pop tunes might loosen her up. And Joan Prentice has some nerve, complaining. I used to get terrific tips for singing 'I Ain't Down Yet.' Tons of applause, too."

Yep, Mom was definitely considering getting back into the clubs again. She talks about it whenever she gets disgusted teaching piano. Luckily, she's never followed through.

Mom doesn't make tons of money teaching, but since she does it six days a week, often eight hours a day, we do all right. The prospect of her entertaining in clubs and coming home at three A.M. again seemed lousy to me.

"I'll copy some new flyers for you," I offered. "I bet you'll have a new student within a week."

To cheer Mom up, I offered to make dinner.

My conversation with Ron about architecture was the inspiration for my kids' next art lesson. After they'd finished painting the clay models they'd made at our last lesson, I dumped a box filled with scraps of fabric, glue, and colored papers onto the floor. We always sat in a back corner of the Prince George lobby. Once I'd asked the management to supply a work table, but they'd said it was against their rules. I bring an old sheet and lay it out so the kids and I won't have to sit on the filthy floor.

Sonja sat cross-legged, staring excitedly at the colorful bits and pieces as they cascaded from the box. "Pretty."

"I want you all to design yourselves a room to live in," I told them. "These papers and fabrics can represent furniture."

Antoine sneered. "More sissy shit."

"Not if you design yourself a macho room," I said.

"If I had my own room," said Monty, "I'd have one whole damn wall with the biggest damn TV you ever saw."

I pushed some papers toward him. "Design it." I cut out various shapes. "See, these rectangles can be sofas or beds."

"Maybe the squares can be tables," said Antoine.

"That's right. And what will the circles be?"

"Candy," said Sonja, giggling. "Big bowls of candy. In my room I want lots of candy."

"Too much candy rots your teeth," said Mitchell (which is more than he usually contributed verbally). He grabbed his share of supplies and retreated into his accustomed corner.

Nearby, a heavyset Latin woman stood pushing a stroller back and forth. The child strapped inside looked about three years old—too old for such restriction. At first I'd thought kids tied up this way were being mistreated by their mothers. Actually, most mothers do it to prevent their little kids from crawling around on the ground. They're afraid they'll pick up dirt, cigarette butts, broken glass, and empty crack vials. Unfortunately, being tied up so much slows down a kid's development. These three-year-olds often can't walk properly. There's no safe place for them to crawl around inside the hotel, and the nearest park is far away. Welfare mothers are often afraid to sit in playgrounds with "normal" mothers anyway, because they have no self-confidence.

I smiled at the toddler, but he didn't smile back. That's typical, too. Lots of the little kids can't express emotions.

His mother smiled at me, though, and I smiled back. "When he's a little older he can join our art class," I said. I asked Sonja to translate for me, since I don't speak Spanish. When I started high school, I'd chosen French as my language. I suppose I thought I'd be spending my summers in Paris studying art. Real stupid. It would've been more practical to take Spanish—something I could actually *use*.

"The lady, she says thank you," Sonja told me. "She says when she brings her baby down here, he don't cry so much."

The woman smiled again, and I nodded.

"My baby sister, she always cries," Sonja added. "Sometimes she cries all night."

I didn't know much about my kids' personal lives. For them, my visits were special, so they didn't waste time talking about everyday life. All I knew about Sonja was that she lived with her mother, who was very young, and her baby sister, who was very sickly. Sonja's mother spent lots of time rushing the baby to the emergency ward or visiting her in the hospital. Monty had taken Sonja under his wing. He'd adopted her as his little sister. This worked out fine for them both, because Monty needed someone to look up to him.

Sonja was designing her room with such intensity that tiny beads of perspiration began clustering on her forehead and moisture clung to the shiny black ringlets framing her face. Her deep brown eyes were riveted on her work until she was satisfied with the results. "I finished," she said proudly. "Want to see my room?"

"Sure. Tell us all about it."

Sonja moved her finger over the spots where she'd glued down multicolored confetti snips. "These are the flowerpots," she explained enthusiastically. "There's lots and lots of flowers." Then she placed her finger on her lips dramatically. "Sssh, be quiet. Don't make no noise inside my room." She drew our attention to the patch of pink taffeta she'd glued over a paper rectangle. "That's my bed. It's so big; it's the biggest ever." Then she pointed to another clump of pasted multicolored paper. "These are all my toys. I'm so rich, I have almost ten toys."

"It looks beautiful," I said. "Is it a big room?"

Sonja stared at it thoughtfully. "No, it's not big. But it's got lots of flowers. And no one fights, so it's always quiet."

"You designed a wonderful room," I told her.

She had. A huge bed, an abundance of flowers, and silence. Not even Frank Lloyd Wright could improve on that.

# Seven

~~~~~~~~~~

At four o'clock on Tuesday, I began dressing for my date with Ron. I must've changed clothes ten times. I told myself the heat made it hard to know what to wear, but I knew better. I finally settled on my black dress. I told myself I chose it because it's good for ushering, but it's actually the sexiest thing I own.

The minute Mom saw me, she grew curious. "You didn't tell me you had a date tonight."

"Who says I do? I'm just ushering. I'm seeing *Cantorial* at the Lambs Theater."

"Oh? What's it about?"

"Ghosts in a synagogue."

"Sounds grim. When your father and I were dating, there were fun musicals on Broadway."

"It's not a musical. And it's not on Broadway. And who says it's a date?" I asked defensively.

"Nobody," said Mom, smiling smugly. "Have a good time with—whomever."

I took the subway to Forty-second Street. As I walked to the theater, I glanced at my reflection in every shop window because tonight I wanted to look special.

Ron certainly did. He was waiting outside the theater looking handsomer than I'd remembered. Luckily, Leonard wasn't around to comment on Ron's tie, which looked expensive.

"It's such a great night; I walked through the park," he said. "I would've asked you to come along, but I don't know where you live. Listen, what's the catch here? Do you know one of the actors? Or do we sneak in?"

"Neither. We usher. Haven't you ever done it?"

"Nope."

"It's a great way to see an off-Broadway show for nothing. After we've seated everyone, we can sit, too. Unless the house is sold out—then we'll have to stand. Anyway, the price is right."

Ron looked impressed. "I never knew you could do this."

"Not many people do. That's why off-Broadway shows usually need ushers. I called yesterday and made the arrangements."

Helen, the theater manager, was waiting for us in the lobby. She unlocked the theater door and showed us around. Years ago the Lambs Club had been a private theatrical club until the building was bought by a

Baptist church. Now it's the Manhattan Church of the Nazarene. The Lambs Theater, a stately old theater lined in solid oak paneling, is used for their Sunday service and rented out for plays the rest of the week. An interesting combination.

"I've heard stories about this place," said Ron. "I'll bet it has great ghosts."

"Do you like ghosts?" I asked.

"I like good ones. Don't you?"

"Sure," I said, smiling.

I'd once made a mental checklist of things my Mr. Superguy would require. In those days, good looks topped my list, followed by a love of E. B. White, a love of ghosts, and a passion for art and music. Naturally, he'd be honest, committed, and socially conscious. Over the years my list has reversed. Now, social conscience is at the top—but ghosts are still important. Acknowledging ghosts means acknowledging the continuity of life, life beyond life, and the existence of the soul.

Helen showed us the layout of the theater, then assigned the right side to me and the left to Ron. She explained the seat numbers—which were in the center, which on the sides. At first the audience trickled in, so we had lots of time to check their tickets, find their seats, and hand them programs. A few minutes before curtain, though, things sped up. People flooded in a dozen at a time, and it got harder to seat them quickly. They also asked lots of questions about the play—"How long has this been running?" . . . "Is the star of this show the same person who starred in that other thing last year?" . . . etc., etc. I kept smiling and saying, "Sorry, I don't know." But I noticed Ron engaging in some lively conversations on his end, while still managing to seat everyone efficiently. I was impressed.

As the lights went down, Ron hurried toward me. I scanned the house for two empty seats together. There weren't any. There was one in the fourth row on the aisle, another in the sixth row center. "For free, I guess we can't be too choosy," I said as I pushed Ron toward the fourth row.

During intermission, Ron and I had no time to discuss the first act. I was assigned to guard the exit door while Ron gave directions to the rest rooms. After the performance, we picked up the discarded *Playbill* magazines, our final chore of the evening.

When we'd finished, the stage manager draped the set with sheets until the next show. I like watching this part. To me, it's like a continuation of the performance: the unreal is made real, then unreal again. I sat down in one of the seats to watch. As Ron joined me, a black cat appeared from nowhere and jumped into his lap.

"That's Mr. Moon," the stage manager explained. "He lives here. Sometimes he performs here, too. He comes up on stage whenever he likes."

Mr. Moon purred and kneaded his paws as he sat in Ron's lap. "He looks like a stray I once picked up," Ron said. "My mother wouldn't let me keep it. She said it would destroy all the furniture."

I tried to imagine Ron as a little boy, the son of a servant in that huge apartment. "Have you always lived on Fifth Avenue?"

"Always," he said. Then he asked, "Do you like cats?"

"Sure. I love all animals. But I keep too much junk around to have pets. When I was little I sold handmade greeting cards in our lobby and donated the money to an animal shelter. I was real upset when I learned there were so many strays starving on the street. Of course, that was before I discovered some people are in worse shape than animals."

"It sounds like you were a real sincere kid," said Ron admiringly. "I bet you're still involved in social causes—besides feminism, I mean."

"Sure, I'm involved. I give art lessons to a great bunch of kids who live in a welfare hotel. Only I think they teach me more than I teach them. Who knows, maybe I've always been dedicated," I added. "By the way, you were awfully smooth tonight."

"I'm used to socializing with people," he explained.

"But you were so charming."

"I guess I've always been charming," he replied.

"I believe it," I said. I almost blushed.

Helen came down the aisle. "You guys did a great job tonight. Call me again anytime."

Outside, a light summer breeze blew as we walked through the crowded midtown streets.

"How did you like the play?" I asked.

Ron shrugged. "It was okay, not great. What did you think of it?"

"Ditto," I said.

Ron stopped outside a hamburger joint. "Would you like to get something to eat?"

I glanced in the window. Garish plastic Tiffany lamps hung above plastic flowerpots that sat on plastic tables next to plastic chairs. "In there? It's awfully ugly. Besides, the whole joint is nonbiodegradable."

"You're right," Ron agreed. "It's pretty awful. Let's keep walking until we find something better."

As we walked, we discussed the play, Ira Levin, authors in general, and E. B. White in particular, quizzing each other on various lines from his letters.

Before we knew it, we'd walked across town. We were on the East Side standing outside the entrance of the Helmsley Palace Hotel, the twinkling lights encircling its awning.

"Too bad I'm too busted to take you in here for dinner," Ron said.

"I wouldn't be caught dead in there," I said indignantly. "Leona Helmsley can keep her food. She's a prime example of conspicuous consumption, and she gives all women a bad name!"

Ron backed off. "Is another feminist lecture about to hit the fan?"

"No, not feminism; excess wealth and decadence of the rich."

"Tell me," Ron said teasingly, "are you a Communist or a Socialist?"

"I'm a social archivist," I told him. "My art reflects society, and society has lots of problems the rich could help solve. Don't you think so?"

"I think the rich get hit with too many cheap shots. They're not all bad."

Ron's opinion didn't surprise me. After all, his mother works for a super-rich family to whom Ron probably felt he owed loyalty. It was sweet of him. "But we're in this global village together," I argued, "which means everyone should be responsible, including rich people. They consume more, waste more, require more—so they should do more. So should big business. They've got to stop destroying our natural resources to build chemical plants and junk. Every second we lose an acre of trees worldwide. Don't you think that's crazy?"

"Sure it is," Ron agreed. "But big business is helping to cure the problem, too. Sometimes when companies intrude on a natural site, they plant a new forest somewhere else."

"But if they hadn't torn up everything in the first place—"

"Okay," Ron agreed, "they're part of the problem —but they're also part of the solution. And pretty soon, more companies will produce ecologically sound products like fuel-efficient cars. They'll make new fortunes. So don't thumb your nose at big business. Or at the rich, either. As an artist you should realize how much the arts rely on corporate funding and endowments. Rich people have encouraged artistic innovation for centuries. How about that American woman who financed James Joyce most of his life? Without her, he never would've written *Ulysses* or *Finnegans Wake*. And what would this world be without the total incomprehensibility of *Finnegans Wake?* Have you ever read it?"

"A little of it—once. Just a few pages. What are you, anyway, an economist or a philosopher? What're you studying at Harvard?"

"Nothing and everything," Ron said. "I haven't declared my major yet, and they're giving me a tough time. Do you know the primary definition of the word *declare?* To make clear or bright. I wish I could make clear to myself what I want to do."

"Your problem is you're interested in too many things."

"Look who's talking," he said. "You want to change the world all by yourself. And overnight."

"Maybe so, but I can't help it. At the Last Judgment I'll be ready. When it's time to come clean, I'll be prepared."

We'd been so busy talking, we hadn't noticed we were walking downtown again. Without realizing it, we'd come near Grand Central Terminal.

"Look, there's a good example of what I mean," Ron said. "Jackie Onassis helped rescue this landmark when people wanted to tear it down. Sometimes the rich have clout, you know. It's too bad she couldn't do anything to save the Commodore Hotel next door. The Grand Hyatt they replaced it with doesn't have the charm of the old building. It's just glitz and glass, but the Commodore had character. Did you ever see it?"

I laughed at the irony of the question. "Tons of times. My mom worked there as a cocktail pianist."

"No kidding? There aren't too many cocktail pianists around anymore. It must've been fun."

"Not for me," I said. "Mom couldn't always afford a sitter, so sometimes she'd drag me along. I'd fall asleep in a booth or in the kitchen. Do you realize the amount of food thrown out in those places? You'd *have* to develop a social conscience after seeing waste like that, wouldn't you?"

"Would you?"

"I did."

"I bet you were born with a social conscience." Ron stopped and smiled at me. "I wish I'd known you when you were little. I bet you were—intense."

Ron hadn't touched me all evening, so I considered making a move. This would be a great place for our first kiss. I stared up into his eyes. "Like I said, I was real dedicated." But Ron continued walking. He looked at his watch. "I guess it's a bit late to eat. I'd better take you home."

My heart sank. "Okay. The subway isn't far."

We took the shuttle to Times Square. Some Andean musicians were performing in the station, and we stopped to listen. I love Andean flute music. It sounds so sad and ancient; it send shivers through me. Ron had never heard it before.

"I can't believe you haven't discovered these guys," I said. "They perform in the subway all the time. I think they're changing the negative vibes down here and making people a little less crazy."

"All good music should do that," Ron said. "Do you also like classical?"

"I like everything but trumpets and rap."

"Maybe we could go to a concert together some-time," he offered.

"Concerts are too expensive," I told him. "I usually go to rehearsals. You really see what a conductor can do when you attend a Philharmonic rehearsal."

72

When we got off the uptown subway, Ron grew quiet. He didn't say anything as we walked toward Riverside Drive.

When we reached my building, I said, "This is where I live. I'd ask you up but . . ."

"No, it's late, I'd better go. Maybe I can call you about going to a Philharmonic rehearsal."

"I'd like that."

Ron shuffled from one foot to the other awkwardly. "Well, it's been . . . very enjoyable . . . and . . ."

"Stimulating?"

"That's right. It's unusual for me to meet a girl I can talk to—you know?"

"I guess so."

"Well," he said haltingly, "good night, Molly."

He extended his hand. We stood together outside my building and shook hands. Then he waved and walked up the street.

At first I felt stunned and stupid. Then I finally grasped the situation.

Ron Cavendish admired me for my mind—and nothing more.

# Eight

So Ron admired my brain. Was that so terrible? Today my brain, tomorrow something else, maybe.

Anyway, I must've come on like a steamroller with all my outspoken opinions. But I didn't regret it. There are too many problems in the world to waste time being wishy-washy. Right?

When I got upstairs, Mom was already in bed. I knew I was too excited to sleep, so I went into the M.R. to work. I love working late at night. Since I had nothing specific in mind, I rooted through my files. Although the drawers are filled with everything from broken clocks to rusty batteries, I usually know where everything is. What I found took me by surprise.

In a bottom drawer tucked underneath old cans and

boxes lay the first collage I'd ever made. A funny feeling zapped me when I saw it—like when you catch a glimpse of your reflection and don't realize it's you. Sometimes in that split second, you get an objective view of what you're truly like. I remembered what Ron had said about wishing he'd known me when I was little. Sometimes I wish that, too. I mean, it'd be great to go back in time and see myself growing up, you know?

Suddenly the memory of making the collage flooded back. It was the year Dad died, when I was six. I remember Mom and Dad were fighting because he'd come home late after a night of drinking and gambling. They were yelling so loud it woke me up. At first I hid my head under the covers to drown out the sound, but soon curiosity drove me toward the door. I tiptoed into the living room to listen.

"That money was *mine!*" Mom shouted. "I was saving it for a new outfit to liven up the act. I can't get good bookings with ratty clothes."

Dad stumbled toward Mom, grabbed her and kissed her. There was a wild look in his eyes. "You don't need a new dress, you look terrific."

Mom pushed him away. "That won't work anymore."

"C'mon, Claudia, this was a sure thing. I figured we'd double our money."

Mom turned away and stared into the mirror, a blank faraway look on her face. "A red dress, maybe. Red looks dramatic under the spotlight. Red satin, but nothing sleazy."

I turned back to my room. It was the same old argument, and it would get louder before it ended. Each would accuse the other of not caring until the subject got around to me, and they'd attack each other about the lousy job each had done as a parent. I'd already heard it a million times.

I never wanted to hear it again. So instead of returning to my room, I hurried out the back door.

I sat on the steps and closed my eyes.

I had never sat out back before, and when I opened my eyes again I noticed the steps were gray marble and the service elevator door had wired octagonal glass in it and the fire hose attached to the wall was brown and dusty with age. It was exciting to look at ordinary things and really *see* them. I forgot I was upset.

I found some magazines filled with art reproductions stacked by the trash cans. I spread them out and looked through them. The ground was cold, it was very late, and a heavy buzz of silence filled the air as I stared at all the pictures. Lots of them were of sculptures. They appealed to me because they looked like things a child might make. There were wonderful animals made from metal pie tins, coffee tins, and razor blades. I spelled out the name printed underneath them: C-a-l-d-e-r. I liked the pictures so much I ripped them out to keep.

Beside the magazines was a large box filled with castoffs: bits of fabric, eight-track tapes, broken jewelry, old ties, letters, and empty perfume bottles. I started stacking everything in a pile, hoping to make a Calder like the ones I'd seen in the photos, but pretty soon it all came tumbling down.

Anyway, for a while I'd been totally transported to another world.

I was out back for a long time. When I returned inside, the apartment was silent. Mom and Dad had gone to bed. I went back to bed, too, but I couldn't sleep. I kept thinking of those wonderful bits and scraps lying in the trash, so I went back and retrieved them. I was determined to turn them into something.

I dragged all the junk into my room and fiddled with it. Finally, I flattened out the cardboard box, got some paste, and began sticking lots of objects onto the cardboard. In my mind I envisioned it turning into one of those wonderfully whimsical Calders I'd just discovered. I was disappointed when it didn't, but I wouldn't give up. I kept adding things until I'd created a strange assemblage. Exhausted, I finally went to bed.

In the morning Mom found my creation lying on the floor. "Molly, did you make this collage?"

I'd never heard the word *collage*. It sounded very exotic. "Yes. Isn't it pretty?"

"Yes, it's very interesting."

Mom showed it to Dad. I was so pleased when they both agreed I had artistic talent. But before I knew it, they'd started another argument.

Mom was reproachful: "Molly should have art lessons."

Dad was defensive: "We can't afford it."

Mom insisted, "Molly needs real art supplies to work with, not *trash*."

Dad got so angry he began throwing things around. On it went, until I felt guilty for ever having made the darn collage. . . .

As I stood staring at it now, I remembered what Mom had said back then. "If only we had money, Molly's life might be worth something!"

The next day, my friend Elaine called.

"Haven't seen you since the prom," she said.

"I wasn't at the prom, remember?"

"Of course. I still think it was tacky of Isaac to go without you."

"It was *his* prom, Elaine."

"Sure it was, but—well—how have you been?"

It was obvious from the sympathetic tone in Elaine's voice that she felt my life was over without Isaac. Elaine doesn't comprehend temporary relationships. She and her boyfriend, Dwayne, have been an item since junior high. They started going steady because they thought "Dwayne and Elaine" sounded cute together.

"What are your plans for the summer, Molly?"

"I'll be selling my stuff as usual. Summer is my best season."

"Why hassle? With your looks, you can get a cushy job sitting behind a desk in an air-conditioned office."

"I don't want to sit in an office," I told her.

"Know what I think? You're becoming antisocial. Dwayne says lots of artists become antisocial—right before they get eccentric, addicted, or suicidal."

"What are *you* doing this summer?" I asked.

"Dwayne wants us to do an AYH bike tour through New England for two weeks, but I don't know. Those tours are sexually segregated, you know."

"You mean you and Dwayne couldn't sleep together for two weeks?"

78

"I mean I don't know if I want to. I can always get my old job as a mother's helper in the Hamptons. Did you know Isaac is going to Italy?"

"No, I didn't know that."

"Yeah, it was a big surprise. His parents gave him the trip as a graduation present."

I was green with envy. All my life I've wanted to go to Italy. I'm dying to visit the great museums in Florence, Venice, and Siena. I long to see the Botticellis at the Uffizi. "I hope he has a great time."

"I'll bet he'll start pinching all the girls just like the Italians. They say American guys feel compelled to do that when they get there."

"A true cultural experience. Excuse me, I've got to go."

"Okay, but think about what I said, Molly. Seriously."

"About what? My working in an office or my becoming antisocial?"

"Both."

"I'll do that, Elaine. I promise."

I hung up and went into the kitchen, where Mom was having coffee. I was still recovering from Ron treating me like a female eunuch the night before, so I felt surly.

"How was the show about rabbis?" she asked.

"It was about the ghost of a cantor, and it wasn't so great."

"When I was young, the Jewish shows were great," she noted. "Take *Fiddler On The Roof*. I sang 'Sunrise, Sunset' all the time, and my audience loved it. All the shows had peppy numbers."

"And all the world was a stage, right, Mom?"

"Only if you stayed in the spotlight, honey."

I slumped into a chair and sighed. "That means trying to please men, doesn't it?"

"I always pleased myself," she corrected.

"Maybe. But I bet you spent lots of time waiting for Mr. Right to come along."

"Maybe I didn't spend enough," she said. "It's awfully modern to think otherwise, but when I see all these young women trudging off to their almost-important jobs, I wonder what great progress they've made."

"They feel responsible for themselves," I told her. "They're not waiting for some guy to complete them."

"Aren't they?" Mom asked skeptically. As she started to make toast, she noticed the bread had grown moldy so she threw it out. "Lately there's been a strange odor coming from the maid's room. Are you keeping dead rodents in there again?"

"No, it's merely detritus in varying forms."

"That sounds worse."

"I've been collecting wrappers and junk from the garbage outside the Prince George. I'm making a study of what the kids eat."

Mom frowned. "You mean potato peels and things?"

"No way. My kids don't eat anything you have to cook. Cooking isn't allowed."

Mom searched the fridge, then took out some eggs, jam, and another loaf of bread. "Is there such a thing as being too socially significant?" she asked absently.

80

"After all, picking through garbage is pretty drastic."

I sighed with annoyance. "Elaine thinks I'm getting too antisocial and you think I'm getting too socially significant. Personally, I think—" I stared at the food on the table and realized I wasn't hungry. "I think I'll skip breakfast this morning."

"What's wrong?" Mom asked with concern. "Didn't your date go well last night?"

"What's that got to do with anything?" I asked defensively. "Besides, I told you it wasn't a date."

I hurried out of the kitchen and got my selling gear together, plus an odd collection of junk that I planned to use in my next art lesson.

By the time I'd walked halfway through Central Park, I wasn't angry anymore. I'd only been angry at myself, anyway—for not being the type of girl Ron was physically attracted to.

The day was slightly gray and overcast. Outside the museum, potential customers gathered around my display, but no one seemed in the mood to buy. Finally a well-dressed woman picked up my seashore nature collage. I'd included various specimens of endangered shore life. She stared at it for a long time, then asked, "How long did it take you to make this?"

Frankly, I think that's a stupid question that has nothing to do with art. A person might take a lifetime to paint a picture that might still be putrid, right? So who cares? Everyone, apparently, because everyone asks.

I had no idea how long it took me, so I lied. "Four

and a half days," I told her. "It took me exactly four and a half days."

That impressed her. "Really? I'll take it."

With a sale finally under my belt, I asked the couple selling next to me to watch my table a minute while I made a phone call. I wanted to apologize to Mom for getting angry.

"Sorry I blew up at breakfast," I told her.

"You didn't have any breakfast," she said with motherly concern. "I hope you didn't think I was insulting your artwork, Molly. I'd never do that. All artists must be totally free to express themselves."

"No, Mom, it was my fault. Know what I found in the M.R. last night? The first collage I ever made. Do you remember it?"

"Of course I do. That's when your father and I first realized how talented you are. We were so proud."

Snatches of the argument Mom and Dad had about me popped into my mind again. "It was fun to see it again. I didn't know I still had it."

"Goodness knows what else is in that room," Mom said.

"By the way," I said haltingly (getting around to the second reason I'd called), "I was wondering if anyone tried to reach me this morning. Did I get any calls?"

"No, Molly, no calls."

I sighed. There'd been the slightest chance Ron might've given me a ring. "Okay. Thanks, Mom. I'll see you tonight after I visit my kids. Finding that collage gave me a great idea for their art lesson."

"Be careful down at that awful place," Mom cautioned—as always.

When I arrived at the Prince George, all my kids were waiting in the lobby—except Mitchell, who hung to one side as usual.

Sonja's eyes lit up when she saw me. She could hardly wait for me to open the shopping bag. But as I dumped things on the floor, her face turned sullen. "Where's all the pretty colors?"

"I didn't bring crayons or paints this time. I brought something more interesting."

The kids glanced at the crushed cans, paper clips, coat hangers, empty takeout cartons, old corks, bottle caps, and typewriter ribbons.

"That's crap from the garbage," said Monty.

"Sure, but I bet you guys can turn it into something great," I told him.

"No way, I ain't gonna be touchin' that shit," said Antoine. "It'll give me AIDS or somethin'."

"This is safe garbage," I assured him. "I brought it from home."

Sonja frowned. "I don't want your garbage."

"But nothing's really useless," I told her. I took out my book about Calder and showed them the pictures. "This man turned ordinary objects like these into great art. Alexander Calder never worried if he had no money for expensive supplies. He knew he could make beautiful art anyway. Don't you want to try it, too?"

"I don't like garbage," Sonja repeated.

"Pretend it's not garbage," I said. "Calder didn't

83

distinguish between art and everyday objects. Once, he made a necklace for his mother from broken pottery and old wire, and it was beautiful. Know what he said? Art should be happy. I bet you can make something really happy from all this. C'mon, you can turn it into something wonderful."

Sonja brightened. "You mean like magic?"

"Right, like magic."

Sonja began poking through the objects, looking for the most colorful ones.

"I still say it's shit," said Monty. "Ain't no one gonna look at stuff made from junk."

"You're wrong," I told him. "Alexander Calder got rich making things from junk. He's very famous." I handed the book to Mitchell, who quietly turned the pages. "Right now there's a big exhibit of Calder's work at a museum."

Sonja selected the red and black typewriter ribbon. She rolled it out across the floor.

Antoine got mad. "Ain't we good enough for you to bring us good stuff?"

"I use this stuff all the time, only I look at it through an artist's eyes. You can do that, too." I handed Sonja some cardboard and glue. "What can you make with that old ribbon? What's it look like?"

Sonja twisted the ribbon into different shapes. "It looks sort of like a snake, I guess."

"Very good," I encouraged her, thrilled something else had come into her mind besides a rainbow. "Okay, this is your version of a snake." I watched her paste it down. "Can't you see it slithering through the gooey swamp? Where are its eyes?"

She looked through the pile and selected two pieces of cork. "Now he can *see* me," she said, giggling.

Monty finally got in the swing of it. He took some paper clips and metal hangers and twisted them into an airplane. Eventually Antoine joined in, too. Mitchell continued looking through the Calder book.

"The museum I mentioned is called the Cooper-Hewitt," I explained. "There are lots of Calder's things on exhibit there. I'd like to take you all to see them."

As usual, no one accepted my offer, but I hoped they were thinking about it.

Later that night the phone rang, and Mom answered. "It's the unfamiliar voice of an unfamiliar young man," she said coyly, handing me the receiver. I waited until she was out of earshot.

"Hello?"

"Hi, it's Ron. How are you?"

"I'm okay. How are you?"

"Fine. I thought you might like to go to a concert—I mean a rehearsal. I've got two tickets for the Philharmonic tomorrow morning at Avery Fisher Hall."

"Really? That sounds great. I've got a gallery appointment downtown at three, but I'm free until then. What's on the schedule?"

"Schubert's Fifth Symphony. Zubin Mehta is conducting."

"Fabulous."

"Yes, all the girls love Zubin. But I suspect it's strictly a sex thing. To most of them he's just another pretty face."

I wondered how many girls he had discussed Zubin

Mehta with. I tried to act casual, not wanting him to realize how I was panting to see him again. "What else are they playing?"

"Mendelssohn's Violin Concerto. Do you know it?"

"Sure I do. Who's the guest soloist?"

"Itzhak Perlman. Are you interested?"

"Sure."

"Good. It starts at nine-thirty."

"Okay, I'll meet you in the lobby of Avery Fisher Hall at nine-fifteen."

Silence. Then Ron said, "Do you always make all the rules?"

"Sorry, did you want to meet someplace else? Earlier maybe?"

"No, that's okay. See you there."

I could hardly wait!

# Nine

In the lobby of Avery Fisher Hall, the Friends of the Philharmonic were serving coffee and Danish to subscribers. When no one was looking, I grabbed two Danish and stuffed them in my bag. "For intermission," I explained.

"I didn't know you were a subscriber," said Ron.

"What's it matter? These'll be in the garbage later, and I don't believe in waste."

"Part of your social salvaging?"

We both laughed as we hurried into the auditorium.

Most of the seats were already taken. The front rows are reserved for subscribers, and other seats get snatched up early by old ladies who wait on line for ages.

"We should've come earlier," Ron said.

"Relax, I never come early. Did you know the average American spends four and a half years waiting on line? Anyway, the front seats aren't the best. I made an acoustical study of this theater, and I like the third row from the back." I noticed two empty seats there. "C'mon."

"Maybe you should write a survival guide to the city," Ron suggested as he followed me. We sat down and listened to the orchestra tune up. "It's hard to believe so many diverse sounds will eventually come together."

"Zubin will soon get them under control," I told him.

The program began with the Schubert symphony. The orchestra played it through once, then Mehta returned to the weak spots to work out the problems. Hearing the conductor's comments is my favorite part of the rehearsal. I love to learn how things are structured. But Ron was getting impatient.

"There are always lots of interruptions," I explained. "Haven't you ever been to a rehearsal before?"

Ron slumped into his seat. "Never. But I'll get the hang of it."

I suddenly realized Ron must've gotten rehearsal tickets especially for *me*.

During intermission, we ate the stolen Danish and discussed the mystique of various conductors.

"All conductors are incredibly sexy," I said, "even when they're old. And they all live to be a hundred."

"It's probably their total power," Ron suggested. "That keeps them young. It must be great to be in complete control like that. I suppose everyone has imagined himself leading an orchestra. I bet it's a little like being God. Maybe that's what St. Joan was seeing in her vision."

"You think so?"

"Sure. I bet Joan is seeing a vision of God as a conductor."

I smiled, remembering our time together in the museum. "Maybe. Or maybe that's your own personal fantasy. Would you really like to conduct an orchestra?"

Ron threw me a quizzical glance. "What're we playing now? The fantasy game?"

"Why not? Would your fantasy be to conduct?"

"No, I don't think so. But it might involve music."

"So tell me," I said with interest.

"Not yet. Maybe when I've known you a little longer."

I glanced at the program. "You didn't tell me they'd be playing Ravel's *Bolero*, too."

"Well—you know what they say about Ravel's *Bolero*."

"What?" I asked coyly. "It says here in the program it was meant to be a ballet for orchestra."

"It's also supposed to be great musical accompaniment during sex," Ron added. "I learned that watching Bo Derek in the movie *10*. Ironically, I happened to be ten at the time."

I'd heard that about the *Bolero*, too. "We feminists don't acknowledge the existence of Bo Derek," I said lightly.

After intermission, the guest soloist, Itzhak Perlman, played the Mendelssohn to perfection. The E-minor concerto is an emotional roller coaster for me: both wildly romantic and deeply sad. Mehta waved his baton and Itzhak played his heart out. I felt strangely excited, too, as if at any moment I might fall off a cliff or something. There was nothing safe and predictable about Ron, the way there had been with Isaac.

When Mehta began conducting Ravel's *Bolero*, I got real self-conscious. Zubin must've heard that story about the *Bolero* a million times. He started slow and steady. Gradually the music swept up and entered into me like waves as it rose to crescendos and—well, you get the picture. Toward the middle, I began imagining Ron removing every stitch of my clothes and tenderly kissing my entire body.

When it was finished, Mehta made the orchestra repeat it several times. I squirmed in my seat. How much more could I take?

Ron leaned over and whispered, "What are you thinking?"

"I think I'm getting hungry," I told him.

"Do you want to stop somewhere for lunch afterward?"

I wanted to *be* his lunch! "No, I brought sandwiches. I hope you like egg salad."

We took the sandwiches to Central Park. We passed Tavern on the Green, then decided to visit the Central Park Zoo.

"I'm so glad they remodeled this place," I said, glancing out over the snow monkey island. "Lions and elephants don't belong in cages inside the city. It's so inhumane."

"I agree," Ron said. "This new zoo shaped up well. No cages, just environments."

"People say someday the only place we'll see wild animals like elephants will be inside zoos," I said. "They're becoming extinct because of the ivory poachers, but I don't know who's buying all that illegal ivory."

"The Middle East buys lots of it," Ron explained. "Ivory-handled daggers are still considered very macho over there. Most poor African nations can't fight back. They don't have enough money for ammunition to fill the rifles to ward off the poachers. Poachers only kill the older elephants, and that leaves the babies orphaned. Sometimes they're brought to elephant shelters because they develop psychological problems when they're left alone, just like children."

"Did you ever read *Leaves of Grass* by Walt Whitman? I think I agree with him about animals. I'd rather live with animals than people."

Ron nodded. "Straight Walt, that's what E. B. White called *Leaves of Grass*."

"Sometimes I wonder who the superior beings on this planet actually are," I said bleakly. "They don't seem to be humans."

"Dolphins, maybe?" Ron suggested. "Many people think dolphins are actually extraterrestrials—like angels."

"If that were true, the poor things wouldn't get slaughtered in tuna nets."

"Which animal would you most like to be?" he asked.

"One of those sea lions," I said, pointing toward their tank. "They're free-spirited, always happy, always clean, and always friendly."

Ron and I sat on the bench beside the transparent tank and watched the sea lions shoot up into the air, then dive back down into the water. Each time they popped up, their shiny skins glistened in the sunlight.

I unwrapped the sandwiches. "I've known you at least an hour longer now. Why don't you tell me your fantasy?"

Ron picked up a sandwich. "Egg salad, that's great. When I was little I ate egg salad every day for lunch. Egg salad or tuna fish."

"Quit evading the question," I insisted. "Come clean with your fantasy."

"Not unless you promise you won't laugh," he said nervously.

"No guarantees. Tell me anyway. Or is it too kinky for mixed company?"

"Okay," said Ron, "I guess I can't get off the hook. It involves Ann Reinking. When I was a kid, I saw her in *All That Jazz*."

"Did you spend your entire childhood watching sexy movies?" I asked teasingly. "Was this before or after your experience with Bo Derek?"

"Do you want to hear this or not?"

"Sure. Tell me more."

"In this fantasy, I'm walking down the street and I meet Ann Reinking. She's sobbing hysterically, so I

92

ask her what's wrong. Then she suddenly throws herself into my arms. She tells me she's performing that night, but her partner just broke his leg. It's some big benefit to raise tons of money for some disease, so she can't miss it. But she has no one to dance with her. So I offer to fill in and be her partner. That's when she brings me to this deserted old rehearsal hall."

"Now comes the kinky part?"

"We start to dance together. To her amazement—and mine, too—I dance like Baryshnikov. I guide her across the floor, and we glide around together as if my feet have wings. Then she tells me she has never danced with anyone who thrilled her so much in all her life. That night, we do the show together and we're a huge success—uncontrollable applause. Afterward, she waves good-bye to me, and I dance out of her life, never to see her again."

"That's it?" I asked disappointedly. "You just dance together? That hardly seems earth-shattering. Not even impossible. I mean, it sounds like something that might conceivably happen."

Ron laughed. "Me dance like Baryshnikov? Never in this life! Whenever I try to dance, I feel like someone nailed my feet to the floor."

"It still sounds like a reserved fantasy to me," I told him.

"And yours is earth-shattering, I suppose? Okay, what is it? No, don't tell me, let me guess. You're like Stuart Little—you want to be Chairman of the World."

"I don't always have to be in charge," I argued. I glanced toward the sea lion tank. Lots of little kids were squealing with delight as they watched the antics of its inhabitants.

"Actually, my fantasy involves those sea lions," I confessed. "I think they like our company as much as we like theirs. Sometimes I watch them from over the park wall after the zoo has closed. On my way home from selling, you know. When everyone leaves, I think they look lonesome. So in my fantasy I imagine myself as the person who visits them all the time—rain or shine. I stand and watch them even when it's pouring out—even at night. And sooner or later the zookeeper notices me. He realizes I'm not just a fair-weather friend. One rainy day when there's no one else around, he takes pity on me. He sees me watching in the rain and offers to let me throw the sea lions their fish. He even allows me to get inside the tank with them and swim around. There I'd be, swimming around with those sea lions, staring up into the trees and the high-rises along Fifth Avenue. Wouldn't that be fantastic?"

Ron took my hands. "You sound just like Holden Caulfield. Are you sure you didn't read that in *The Catcher in the Rye?*"

I pulled away. "Are you making fun of me?"

Ron took the last bite of his sandwich. "No, but I wouldn't call your fantasy earth-shattering, either."

"Maybe not," I agreed. "but I've always dreamed of swimming with sea lions."

"Sorry. I guess I thought your fantasy might involve women's lib or something."

"I guess I come on a bit strong with that. But we've got so much catching up to do! Society is still steeped in prejudice, you know."

"Is a lecture headed my way?" Ron asked.

"Maybe just a short one," I warned him. "The other night on TV I saw some kids being interviewed about religion. They were asked what God looked like. Everyone described God as a sweet old man in flowing white robes and a long beard. When they were asked why no one described God as a woman, one little girl said, 'Because God isn't a girl's name.' See what society does? It stops us before we begin."

Ron stared into my eyes and smiled. "If you weren't so serious, you'd be perfect." I looked away. "I thought we might see an art exhibit together," he added. "The Cooper-Hewitt has a Calder show, which should interest you. Have you seen it yet?"

"No, I was hoping to take Mitchell, one of my kids at the welfare hotel. I'll bet he's never been inside a museum, only I know he won't come with me."

"Then I can be your second choice, okay?"

"Sure, as long as it's a . . ."

"I know, a free Tuesday night, right?"

"Am I too pushy?"

"The thought never occurred to me." As we threw our sandwich wrappings in the trash, Ron said, "C'mon, let's visit the tropical birds."

"Okay, but going in there always reminds me of how the real rain forest is being destroyed. An acre a second, did I tell you?"

"Yes, you did," Ron said, pulling me toward the entrance.

Inside, the air was humid and sultry. Tiny multi-colored birds flew high above the semicircular ramps and darted through the leaves of the giant palm trees growing along either wall. Water cascaded down the falls set against the sides. Turtles and crocodiles plodded through the narrow stream, while snakes crawled along the mossy rocks.

The place was almost empty—only two people strolling on one of the ramps above us. As we walked along, Ron drew me close to him and whispered in my ear. "I thought about you all last night. And the night before."

"Really? I thought you'd forgotten me."

"You're not a forgettable person, Molly."

"I guess I thought you weren't interested."

"You were wrong," he said, beginning to stroke my back in a circular motion. "I'm finding it real hard to keep my hands off you."

Now that Ron had finally made a move, I felt torn. I was afraid I'd get carried away. I've always saved really passionate emotional stuff for my art. I wasn't sure I was ready to transfer it into a sizzling relationship, which I sensed was the only kind I could possibly have with Ron. I hurried ahead of him, glancing up at the palm trees. "Trees are marvelous things. They take carbon dioxide out of the atmosphere and put—"

Ron caught up to me and pulled me toward him. Then he kissed me. The kiss—long, hard and searching—sent warm waves through my whole body. "I can't get you out of my mind," he whispered. He kissed my cheeks, my eyes, my neck. "I'm not sure what's happening."

I kissed him back. Again and again. Suddenly, everything around me began slipping away. All I was conscious of was a longing inside. Holding him close, I said, "I don't think I've ever felt this way. Does that sound sappy?"

"No," he whispered, "I never have, either. C'mon, let's go someplace more private."

Where could we go? His apartment, I hoped. Was Ron allowed to have visitors at the home of Mr. and Mrs. Worthington Spratt II? Did he often bring girls there? I didn't care where we went as long as we could be alone together. That was all I could think of.

I followed him down the ramp and out into the sunshine.

As we walked toward the exit of the zoo, a beautiful girl dressed in riding britches walked by. She glanced at Ron, stared at me—then back at Ron again as if she'd discovered him with a two-headed mutant. Sophisticatedly casual, she pushed her shiny blond hair from her face. "Ron, is that really you? When did you get back?"

She and Ron hugged each other. "Hi, Francie," he said, "I've been home a few days."

"Impossible," she insisted. "I haven't seen you in your usual haunts. You must be in hiding."

I took an instant dislike to snooty Francie-poo. And I couldn't help wondering where Ron's "usual haunts" might be.

Ron didn't bother to introduce us.

"Keep in touch," said Francie as she waved and walked away.

"Very horsey," I noted, watching her go.

"Yes, she's a great rider," said Ron.

"She looks it."

"I'd rather not discuss Francine just now."

Ron put his arm around my waist, then stroked my upper arm with his fingertips. A tingle ran through my entire body. "Let's get out of here. You're very special, Molly Malone. I want to be alone with you." He kissed my neck. "You have the same hair color as the model in all of Rossetti's paintings. In fact you're very Pre-Raphaelite, Molly. The sumptuously ideal woman." He began nibbling my ear. But Francie-poo's appearance had broken the mood.

"I think I have to go now," I said.

Ron looked startled. "Go? But why? I thought . . ." He stared ahead, in the direction Francie had gone. "Is it because of . . ."

"It's because we're going too fast," I told him. "I'm not totally sure what's happening here, and I'd rather not do anything stupid. I think we'd better slow down."

"It may be too late for that," Ron said, kissing me again.

"Anyway, I've got an appointment."

"Cancel it."

"Are you kidding? It's with a gallery director—one of those people who never see humans. I told you we'd only have half a day together."

"But it hasn't been enough," Ron argued, then nibbled my ear again. "Okay. As long as we still have our date for Tuesday night."

"The Calder show? Sure. We'll meet early and walk through the park."

"Don't I ever get to be boss?"

"Sure, someday. When you take me to the big dance, I'll let you lead."

"With my two left feet?"

Ron walked me to the bus stop. We kissed several times, and each time I felt a buzz shoot up through my toes. Then he waved good-bye as my bus pulled out.

# Ten

I was filled with such a mixture of contradictory emotions, I was glad to put them all on hold and return to thinking about my work.

When I got home, I picked up my portfolio then took the subway down to Soho. During the ride I tried to push Ron out of my mind, but he kept popping back in.

Did he really think I was special? Was I ready for what might happen between us? Was I turning into a sap? Already, I didn't like the totally mushy feeling I got whenever I was close to him—like I wasn't in control. And I like to be in control.

I got off at Canal Street and walked past the electrical supply, army/navy surplus, and used clothing stores. I often find interesting things there at bargain prices, but today I didn't feel like shopping so I walked straight toward Broome Street.

I've always liked the funky blend of old warehouses, cobblestone streets, and trendy shops in Soho, although lately things have grown a little too trendy. The shops are crawling with the scent of piñon incense, and the windows are filled with Santa Fe–style furniture. Suddenly the once-modest little art galleries are now taking in big money, so new galleries pop up almost overnight.

This one, called the Edgewater Gallery, had Corinthian columns outside the turn-of-the-century building. Inside, the exhibit area still smelled of its newly painted walls and the highly varnished parquet floor. The place looked deserted. A receptionist sat in the anteroom. He was young, attractive, and well dressed. I hoped he wouldn't turn out to be the type who considered himself part of the art world intelligentsia and yet had no consideration for artists. "May I help you?" he asked with a weak, condescending half smile.

"I have an appointment to show my slides to Mr. Hathaway."

He seemed surprised. "Really? Normally, Mr. Hathaway doesn't see artists. We request that you mail in your slides."

Oh yes, I knew his type: haughty and bitter. Artists off the street were less than dirt under his feet. His response triggered a knee-jerk reaction in me. I remembered the treatment I'd received at the hands of such receptionists before, and I grew angry. "No kidding? Well, maybe Mr. Hathaway wasn't feeling normal the day he talked to me. I've got an appointment. My name's Molly Malone." I said.

"Wait here one moment," he said as he knocked on the director's door.

While I waited, I checked out the art exhibit already mounted in the gallery. It showcased an artist overly fond of pink. There was one nauseating pink canvas after another, either punctuated or encrusted with fragments of Ping-Pong balls, all in the bilious color of Pepto-Bismol. I noticed a red dot beside one, signifying it was sold. The price was twenty thousand dollars. I nearly threw up! At first glance, Edgewater looked like lots of the glitzy new super-trendy places where what's hottest and newest is more important than what's best. Trying not to prejudge, I decided to reserve my opinion until I'd met the director. After all, he was one of the few who had agreed to meet me in person.

Martin Hathaway, the director, greeted me. "Miss Malone? I only have five minutes." He escorted me into his office, then opened my portfolio. One by one, he placed my slides on the light box. His face was expressionless. When he'd finished looking at my slides he asked, "Anything else?"

"That represents a year's work," I told him.

He stared at me blankly. "Anything else?"

"Maybe you'd like to take a closer look?" I took one of my slides and replaced it on his light box. It was my crack vial collage. Underneath the used vials, I had mapped out their route from the vials' manufacture in Taiwan to being smuggled into the U.S., and from there to the crack retailers and onto the streets of Manhattan.

102

He barely gave it a second glance. "Yes, shades of Dada—more political, actually. Very intense. But we don't judge work here, Miss Malone; we merely showcase it. Edgewater wishes to reflect the existing art market. Do you feel you know the existing art market?"

Should I tell him what I *really* thought? That all galleries—although necessary evils for an artist—are merely players in a decadent game filled with sad irony, malice, and conceit. That today's commercialized so-called art world is actually a world of *piranhas*. "Maybe not," I replied.

"Perhaps that's the problem," he agreed, checking his watch. "Good day, Miss Malone."

As Mr. Hathaway smoothly dismissed me from his office, I watched him suddenly transform into an amalgam of the dozens of gallery owners who'd looked down their noses at my stuff in the past. Like the receptionist, he had become a symbol: the receptionist and the rejectionist. What a pair!

"On the other hand," I quickly added, "maybe I don't want to produce lobby art that matches the corporate furniture. Or maybe I think you have rotten taste. And maybe you do, judging from the inferior work that's hanging in your gallery!"

Seemingly unperturbed, Martin Hathaway handed me back my portfolio. "I wish you luck placing your work elsewhere. Now, if you'll excuse me."

Before I knew it, I was out the door.

I didn't look back, but I was darn sure that snooty receptionist was sneering.

Okay, so diplomacy isn't my middle name. As I

walked back to the subway, I tried to figure out why I had exploded.

It didn't take me long to figure it out. While I was busy being turned down at Edgewater, I could have been with Ron.

Tuesday seemed like a long way off.

# Eleven

~~~~~~~~~~

When I got home, I saw that Mom had dumped everything out of the hall closet. Boxes, bags, and suitcases lay scattered all over the floor.

"What are you doing?" I asked, sensing something was up. "Shouldn't you be giving a piano lesson?"

"Brett Coburn has chicken pox," she explained, standing in the center of the mess she'd created.

"I can't find my evening bag. I had a charming beaded bag in one of these boxes, and now I can't find it. Those bags have come back into style lately. Lots of my old clothes are in again, isn't that lucky? And I've only gained two pounds in ten years, so everything will fit nicely."

Mom removed a plastic garment bag from the closet.

As she unzipped it, a patch of green satin flashed from the opening.

"Why do you need that old dress?"

Mom carefully slipped it from the bag. "Isn't it beautiful? Can you imagine what a dress like this would cost today?"

I watched her fluff up the skirt. "Why are you dragging that out?"

Mom looked annoyed. "I told you, I'm thinking of getting back into the business. With so many posh new hotels, I'll get a job in a snap."

"Why now, all of a sudden?"

Mom removed a slip of paper from her skirt pocket. "This is our new rent increase. Pretty soon it might be more than we can afford—unless I rent out the maid's room."

"Not my M.R! You can't do that, Mom."

"Relax, maybe it won't be necessary." Mom held the dress up to herself. She glanced in the mirror while she swirled around the room. "All I need is a few good gigs to get me going again. That shouldn't be too hard, should it?"

"I don't know, Mom," I said bleakly.

Then I went into the M.R. and closed the door.

I didn't like seeing that dress again. It was a copy of the one Rita Hayworth wore in the movie *Gilda*: strapless with a big bow on the side.

When Mom was a kid in the Fifties, she had seen *Gilda*, as part of a Rita Hayworth retrospective. Mom thought she was the sexiest woman alive. In her act,

Mom always wore her hair the way Rita did, with soft curls cascading down her shoulders. Sometimes she'd sing "Put the Blame on Mame" (minus the striptease). By then, it was already kitschy nostalgia, but Mom didn't care. I think she sometimes imagined she actually *was* Rita Hayworth. When she married Dad, she probably saw herself marrying her handsome prince like Rita had done when she married Aly Khan.

Much later, when Rita Hayworth died of Alzheimer's disease, Mom went into mourning. "I read that no one ever came to visit her," Mom said. "Everyone in Hollywood had forgotten Rita. Only her daughter, Yasmin, stood by her."

The day Rita's death was announced, Mom dug out her old *Gilda* movie still. She bought one white rose and placed it on the mantel beside the photo. She wrote a note that said, "We all love you. And we all miss you."

It made me cry. But I wasn't crying for Rita Hayworth. I was crying for Mom. A tiny wisp of life floated out of her that day, like a dandelion puff blown away in a breeze.

I remembered the first time I'd seen Mom wear the dress. She was seated at the piano, a soft pink spotlight accenting her auburn hair and flooding across her shoulders. Mom had a lovely neck and shoulders, but she never wore any jewelry to show them off. "Skin is much sexier than jewels," she would tell me. "Besides, if a gentleman thinks you have no jewelry, he's more likely to provide you with some." Mom would always throw me helpful little hints like that while I watched her prepare to go on—all the things a young lady needed to know to snag a rich eligible man—such as: "Always powder your feet before you put on your stockings. It keeps your nylons from snagging." Mom regarded these pearls of wisdom as necessary additions to my elementary education. To her distress, I have never taken her advice regarding snagging men *or* nylons.

But at the time, I listened to every word. Watching Mom prepare was always exciting. Sometimes on rainy nights we would get to the hotel early so Mom could change her clothes in the powder room. Mom loved the hotel's powder room. It had upholstered lounges, marble walls, and soft lighting. "Good lighting brings out a lady's finer points," she would tell me. Mom imagined this was her own private dressing room, so she always considered the women coming in an intrusion. "I suppose they have to go *someplace*," she'd mutter begrudgingly, putting the final touches on her makeup.

Then we'd go into the restaurant. Before the dinner hour, it was usually empty, so I'd watch the waiters prepare the tables. Mom would prop up her eight-by-ten glossy (a photo in which she closely resembled Rita) on the piano. Then she'd test out the keys before beginning the five sets she would play between seven and midnight. She'd place an empty brandy snifter beside her photo. "This new dress should help pick up tips."

"You look beautiful, Mommy," I'd say.

"Pray I won't have to fight to get them tonight, honey."

Mom usually had to perform over people who noisily clinked their silverware and glasses, and sometimes the manager would tell her, "Don't play so loud, it bothers people when they eat."

Around nine o'clock, Mom would hit her stride, but by then I was usually getting tired. A waiter would set up a tiny table for me in the corner near the kitchen. I was always very quiet because technically I wasn't supposed to be there. But Mom had charmed the maître d' into allowing me to stay by explaining she couldn't afford a sitter. Sometimes I'd put down my head and take a nap, unless loud noises from the bar woke me up.

One night two guys who'd had too much to drink were laughing and gesturing at Mom as she finished her set. I saw right away what they thought was so funny. Mom was seated on the raised stool behind the piano, wearing her strapless gown. From their vantage point, it looked like she was *naked*. When Mom did her final number, "I Ain't Down Yet," they rushed over and dumped several dollar bills in her glass.

Those two guys kept coming back every night for a week—enjoying their grimy little fantasy at Mom's expense. I didn't like watching them watch her. I felt overly protective, as if Mom were the child, not me. Finally, I told her why she was getting such big tips, and I asked her not to wear the dress anymore. She paid no attention. I didn't realize it then, but Mom probably knew how the dress looked, and she didn't care because it got her bigger tips. Mom never told those guys to buzz off because she hoped one of them might be a millionaire.

109

Although millionaires proved rarer than dodo birds, Mom sang and played her heart out five sets a night anyway.

Tell me, who in their right mind would want to return to *that?*

# Twelve

The next day, sitting outside the museum, I kept wishing Ron would pass by, but he didn't.

Around noon, Leonard took a break and joined me.

"Your lunch breaks are becoming a habit," I told him.

"I'm not motivated in my work lately," he explained. "You don't seem too focused yourself."

"No, I was hoping I might see Ron. We had a nice time together yesterday."

"You didn't actually *date* that guy, did you?"

"We went to a Philharmonic rehearsal together, then watched the sea lions and ate egg-salad sandwiches. Would you call that a date?"

"Knowing you, I'd call that your idea of a raging

romance." Leonard looked worried. "Watch out for that guy, Molly."

I tried to see Leonard's real face through his Rempha makeup, but I couldn't. "Quit giving me advice while you're in character. I keep thinking you're smarter than you are."

"I *am* smarter than you about this. I'm warning you, your Ronny is a phony. I don't know his angle, but he isn't what he pretends to be."

"He's not pretending to be anything," I protested.

"Really? What if I told you he's—"

"He's what? Mind your own business, okay?"

"Don't get testy. I was just going to tell you that—"

"Never mind, I won't listen. My private affairs stay private."

"Is it already an affair?" he asked.

I tried to control my anger. After all, Leonard was only being helpful. "I didn't mean to snap at you, but back off, okay? Maybe I'm in a rotten mood today. If so, I'm sorry, but I've got problems."

"What kind of problems?"

"Money problems."

Leonard threw up his hands in a dramatic gesture. "You? Not you who scoffs at such mundane things. You who hath been knowneth to stretcheth a penny for more than a mileth?"

"One and the same," I said. "Mom is making noises about maybe renting out my M.R., which means I may need to make extra money so I can keep it."

Leonard grew silent and looked as if he were turning over some really deep thought in his mind. I mean, he looked like Hamlet wondering whether to *be* or not. Then he said, "I know how you can make some real quick cash."

"How? By selling my body?" I joked.

"Waitressing," said Leonard. "There's a real posh party at the Met on Tuesday night. It's a dinner with a medieval theme, and I'm waitering. I can get Nancy the caterer to give you a gig as a waitress. You've done that kind of work before, haven't you?"

"Sure, sometimes in the winter, I waitress after school. But I don't think I want this gig," I told him. "I don't approve of turning the Western Hemisphere's greatest repository of art into a Rent-a-Palace. I heard they built the Temple of Dendur just so they could have an extra party hall. It's disgusting to let people drop hors d'oeuvres and spill drinks on precious art objects. Besides, I'm busy that night."

"This bash will cost more than a million," said Leonard. "Naturally the Met gets its usual thirty-thousand-dollar rental fee—and you could make a hundred easy."

I didn't go for the idea. "I don't need money that badly. After all, I've got my principles."

"Suit yourself," said Leonard sarcastically. "Being a social archivist, I thought you'd like to observe the upper crust chowing down."

"It's a dinner. Hmm. That means everyone will be eating."

"That's usually true."

"So I could get their garbage." My concept of a

collage comprised of detritus from the Prince George Hotel suddenly blossomed into something far more meaningful and significant. It could be a comparison study of the food eaten by the very rich and the very poor: the castoffs of society's elite as well as of society's castoffs. I loved the idea, and I couldn't wait to see my plan set into motion. "Will the caterers let me take the used wrappers and packaging?"

"Gladly. Most people ask for the flowers."

"Then I'll do it," I decided.

"Okay," he said. "I'll arrange it."

"And I'll cancel my date," I told him.

The day was so slow, I took the afternoon off.

When I got home, I discovered Mom had canceled all her afternoon lessons. She had dragged out all her pop music sheets and was busy boning up.

I went into the M.R., but I couldn't work. The Edgewater Gallery's rejection lingered like a bad taste in my mouth. I grabbed my portfolio. There had to be some gallery somewhere that wanted my work. One that was neither too trendy nor too conservative—just a little reactionary. And I was determined to find it.

I decided to try Madison Avenue, where lots of newer Japanese-owned galleries have recently opened.

As I walked down the streets, I think I was hoping lightning would strike. When I reached the eighties, I noticed a gallery with a painting by Bastien-Lepage displayed in the window. I thought of *Joan of Arc* in the Metropolitan. Somehow, I felt I'd been guided to this place, even though it didn't look reactionary.

114

Without thinking, I walked in.

Inside, things looked much more traditional than in Soho, and the receptionist was far less hideous. She was an older woman, cold and suspicious maybe, but not snooty. She obviously wasn't used to seeing young people, though. I think she wondered if I'd come to rob the place.

"May I help you?" she asked.

"Do you handle contemporary artists, or only dead ones?"

"What?"

"I'm an artist," I explained. "Does anyone here actually *see* artists?"

Nervously, she pushed her chair away from her desk. "Mr. Shimmerman?" she called out. "Would you please come out here?"

Across the room, a door opened and Mr. Shimmerman appeared. He was in his sixties, with fleecy tufts of white hair and circular spectacles set above the pink rosy cheeks of his benevolent, cherubic face. He slid his little round spectacles down his nose. "Yes, Miss Ogilvy, is there some problem out here?"

I set down my portfolio on the desk. "I'm an artist, and I'd like to show you my slides."

"We rarely see artists," said Mr. Shimmerman. "We have very little space for contemporary art."

Was this one of those super-conservative places that only acknowledge something as art either after it'd been around for fifty years or the artist was dead for a generation—whichever came first? I wasn't sure yet.

I unzipped my portfolio. "I'm sure you'll find this very interesting," I told him.

115

Mr. Shimmerman looked at me with an amused, almost incredulous expression. "Yes—well—all right. Step into my office."

Then Mr. Shimmerman smiled at me, and I felt I had wandered into another time when art galleries were exactly as depicted in Forties films . . . a gallery where an artist's talent was actually nurtured.

It reminded me of the old movie *Portrait of Jennie*, which I'd always loved, especially the scene where the young artist, Eben Adams, enters the Spinney Gallery, cold, hungry, and despondent. Out of sympathy, elderly Miss Spinney buys one of his sketches, then invites him to stay for tea. When he walks out of the gallery, he is warmed inside—renewed, refreshed and inspired—and carries money in his pocket.

I stared at Mr. Shimmerman. Maybe he'd be my Miss Spinney!

As I followed him into his office, Miss Ogilvy stared after us, looking vaguely startled. I felt like telling her she should start brewing the tea.

Mr. Shimmerman had no light box. He held each of my slides out toward the lamp, then carefully replaced it in its slide pocket.

I waited eagerly for his professional opinion.

"What is this?" he asked with interest.

He was pointing to my Cabbage Patch collage. In it, I had used various outfits belonging to Cabbage Patch dolls. "I think dolls who own more clothes than people are obscene, don't you?" I asked. "When I was babysitting Jenny Rosenblum, I traded her all her Cab-

116

bage Patch castoffs for two tickets to a Rangers game someone had given me. I combined the doll clothes with photostats of real infants' death certificates."

Mr. Shimmerman looked closer. *"Death* certificates?"

"I got them from the Department of Health," I explained. "Do you know how many babies die in New York City each year? Anyway, I also included one of those idiotic birth certificates issued to each Cabbage Patch doll the toy factory spawns. See?"

"Yes, I see," he said. "Yes, that's very grim, isn't it? Yet I imagine it's also exciting, working on the cutting edge of art."

I nodded. I was sure this was the moment Mr. Shimmerman would offer to exhibit my work—and then we would sit down to have our tea.

Mr. Shimmerman scratched his head. "Your work has brio but it stops short of parody; that's good. And you have a highly developed sense of design. That's good, too. Do you ever work with old lace?"

"Old what?" I asked.

"Victorian lace," he explained. "Old fans and such things. One artist does quite well with that type of commission. She combines lace with photographs and makes personalized collages for birthdays and anniversaries." Mr. Shimmerman slipped the slide back into its pouch. "I suggest you look into it; it's quite lucrative."

I didn't get his drift. "I beg your pardon?"

Mr. Shimmerman slipped my portfolio underneath my arm. As he led me to the door he gave me a fatherly smile. "You're so young, my dear. Perhaps it's not good to be so serious."

Before I knew what had happened, I was back out on the street with a blast of hot afternoon air smacking me in the face.

In my mind, I went over what Mr. Shimmerman had told me. In his discreet way, he had suggested I forget my principles and sell out.

Thanks a heap, Mr. Shimmerman!

I didn't feel like going home, so I wandered up Broadway instead. Outside the bank on Eighty-sixth Street, I saw my friend Hani, a sidewalk artist, recreating a segment of the Sistine Chapel on the pavement. Sometimes Hani gets so obsessed, he'll work for fifteen hours straight. He makes his own pastels from a combination of chalk, soap, and glue, and when his picture is complete, he sprays it with a fixative so that it lasts for months.

A crowd had gathered around his depiction of the Delphic Sybil, which covered half the block. As Hani's hands made huge sweeping gestures, the street was quickly transformed. A man climbed on top of a phone booth to get a better look and give Hani advice. "More highlights on the nose," he shouted.

Hani smiled and nodded. "That's right, get into it. I love it when my audience gets into the art." He added a bolder stroke along the nose, then got off his knees to stand up and stretch his muscles.

I gestured to him as he picked up the money in his contribution bucket.

118

"Hi, Molly, how are things?" he asked.

"So-so. How's it with you?" I asked.

"Not too bad."

"Have the cops bugged you lately?"

Hani shrugged. "I got arrested last week. I'd been working for twelve straight hours bringing art and beauty to the people, when a cop starts hassling me. He was real nasty, so I got hotheaded. Anyway, when I got to court and the judge heard what I did for a living, he said, 'Who the hell arrested you?'—and he let me off."

"Good for you," I told him.

"And I just got a commission to paint on a canvas," he said proudly.

"No kidding."

"Yeah, some guy came by the other night when I was finishing the Mona Lisa. He wants me to paint his mother."

I stared down at the soft pastel colors of the Delphic Sybil. Her face was more than eight feet wide. Was the original any larger? I wondered. Would I ever get to Rome to find out?

"Why are you so sad today?" asked Hani.

"Am I? I guess I'm just thinking. That's great about your commission. But won't you miss painting on the sidewalk?"

"I'll always paint on the street," he insisted. "Here I'm completely free. As long as there's a pavement, I'll be covering it."

I wondered. If Hani got really famous, would his street art disappear? Was a person better off always struggling but never making it? Was that what kept art pure? Who knew.

A passerby accidentally stepped on Hani's version of the Michelangelo. "Sorry," he said, then he did a mad dance along the sidewalk when he realized what he'd stepped on.

"No sweat," said Hani, quickly retracing the smudged lines of the Sybil's sloping nose. He was hard at work again. "All artists should come to the sidewalk," he said. "It's the best canvas in the world."

When Hani is at peak concentration, he looks like a wild man: a wild mountain man with the streets of Manhattan as his open spaces. He's got it made. The city is his unlimited canvas and every person in it is his audience. He's like an actor playing many parts. He's Vermeer re-creating his beloved Delft, Gauguin on his Tahitian island, Van Gogh in Arles, and Monet at Giverny. He's a magician, too. He makes Botticelli's Venus rise up through the knobby cement pavement and Raphael's Madonna smile enigmatically at people passing by in buses. And each time he paints, he transforms a grimy city street into a wonderland.

As I left, I patted him on the back. "Don't let them tame you, okay? See you around. I hope it doesn't rain."

# Thirteen

I t rained all the next day.
I wonder if God realizes how destructive rain is for street artists, street performers, and street vendors.

We are drowned out!

I tried to resume my work in the M.R., but I couldn't concentrate. I was still recovering from my encounters at the art galleries. I was eager to begin my Prince-George-Hotel-versus-Met-Party collage. But I had to wait to do that, so I tried to be patient.

Since I wasn't selling on the street or working at home, I hoped Ron might call me, but he didn't.

I continued to be patient.

Whenever Mom had a break between classes, she freshened up her old act by adding new songs. I could hear her voice cracking constantly as she accompanied herself while singing "Memories."

I closed the door of the M.R., buried myself in several trashy gossip magazines, then got some art supplies together for my kids' class that evening.

I would catch up on my own work tomorrow.

I woke up extra early the next day and threw on shorts and a T-shirt. The rain had gotten worse. For me, there's nothing gloomier than rainy July days in the city. I call them Devil Days. Ominous dark clouds drape the sky, the air hangs hot and heavy, and I grow a little crazy. I started feeling real nervous inside, like an inmate confined to jail too long. Then I began to feel something terrible was about to happen. So when the phone rang at eight A.M., my heart skipped. I bolted to answer it.

It was Ron. "Sorry to call you so early."

"That's okay," I said, thrilled to hear from him. "What's up?"

Silence.

"What's wrong?" I asked.

"I need to see you. It's important."

"Sure, what's wrong?"

"I can't tell you anything on the phone. Can you meet me at Sixty-fourth and Fifth right away?"

"Not unless I fly. What's the matter?"

His voice sounded urgent. "Get there as soon as you can. Okay?"

"Okay."

"You promise?"

122

"I'm on my way."

I left the house so fast, I nearly forgot to close the door.

I figured something must be wrong with Mrs. Cavendish. Why else would Ron ask me to meet him almost across from where they live? But if that were so, why hadn't he asked me to come to the apartment? I was still trying to figure things out as I hopped into a cab —something I never do unless it's an emergency, and I considered this an emergency. Maybe Ron's mother had slipped and fallen outside their building? But why call me? Didn't they have friends, neighbors? And what about the snooty doorman? Why hadn't I asked for details?

The rain poured down in sheets as the cabby drove through the park. Fog had rolled in, making visibility almost zero so I could barely tell when we'd reached Sixty-fourth Street. Then I saw Ron. He was standing on the corner with one of those huge black umbrellas people always bring to graveyards during rainy funerals.

I dashed out of the cab. "What's wrong? Are you okay? Did something happen to Mrs. C.? What's this all about?"

Ron looked a little sheepish. "Sorry. I didn't mean to make you worry. Everything's okay."

"Then what am I doing here?" I asked.

"Did you really think something was wrong?"

"Sure I did. I don't get many urgent calls at eight A.M."

"And you rushed over? That's very sweet, Molly."

Had Ron been drinking? I wondered. "Have you been to bed yet?" I asked. "What am I doing here?"

As Ron placed his umbrella over my head, an odd furtive expression crossed his face. "I think it's a good time to go to the zoo. There won't be any people there."

"The zoo—are you nuts? It's not even open yet."

"It opens early today," he said as he led me toward the entrance into Central Park.

I started feeling creepy. After all, what did I actually *know* about Cameron Cavendish? He could be an ax murderer! Central Park could be strewn with the bodies of his helpless victims, all neatly buried underneath the trees during early-morning rainstorms. I remembered Leonard had tried to tell me something about Ron, but I hadn't let him. Now I wished I had. "This is weird," I told him. "What are we doing?"

"Haven't you figured it out yet? I thought for sure you would."

"All I can figure is that you're *crazy*."

Ron smiled but didn't say anything. The rain had subsided, but the park was still totally deserted. Not one jogger as far as the eye could see. As we approached the zoo entrance, a keeper met us by the gate.

"We can't go in yet; let's come back later," I said. "The zoo doesn't open until ten."

Ron nudged me through the gate. "It's okay, we'll be finished by ten o'clock."

"Finished with what?"

"For a smart girl, you're real dense," said Ron.

The zookeeper gestured me toward the sea lion pond. "This way. It's good you wore sneakers."

124

I stared down at my sneakered feet. Then I stared at the four buckets of fish resting on the ladder leading into the sea lion tank. "Is he going to feed the sea lions now?" I asked.

Ron smiled. "No, stupid, *you're* going to feed them."

"*Me?* You're kidding."

Ron pushed me toward the ladder. "Move it, Molly Malone: this is your fantasy."

I was thrilled. "You mean you're fulfilling it? How'd you manage this?"

"Hurry up if you're coming," said the zookeeper, "I've got a schedule to keep."

For a moment I felt I was in a dream. I climbed the ladder, picked up the bucket, and walked across the rocks. Almost instantly, a sea lion darted out of the water and crawled across the rocks to greet me. I grabbed a fish and held it toward him. The sea lion cried out, flapped its flippers, then snatched up the fish and gobbled it down.

"Make them work harder for it," the zookeeper shouted. "It gives them more exercise."

As I held a fish up higher, another sea lion approached and smacked me with its flippers. Its skin felt cool and sleekly soft against my leg. "This is wonderful!" I squealed. A sea lion squealed back, then it stared up at me with soulful brown eyes. I smacked my thigh and gestured for it to come closer. It rested its head against my leg and then sucked up several fish. When I sat down on the rocks, all the sea lions approached. One wrapped its flippers around my shoulder. Through a chorus of delightful noises, one by one, they devoured the breakfast I gave them. It felt so great, I thought I'd gone to heaven. There was only one thing keeping this fantasy from being totally perfect. "Can I get in the tank with them?" I asked.

The zookeeper glanced at Ron. "You didn't tell me anything about that."

What had Ron done—bribed this guy? How much had my fantasy cost him?

As the sea lions cavorted around my feet, I stared up at the sky. The gray clouds suddenly parted, allowing a tiny patch of blue to squeeze through. I glanced at Ron, who was now head to head with the zookeeper. Finally, the keeper nodded nervously, then Ron waved to me and shouted, "Okay, go for it!"

I slipped off the rock and slid into the cool water of the sea lion tank. At first, the sea lions seemed startled by the intrusion, but they quickly joined me. They swirled and swam around, butting against one another and including me in their chasing games. I held my nose, dunked my head, and stared at them from underwater. Each one swooped and dived down into the water then up again into the air. As I heard them bark out their happy cries, I felt like a little kid again, playing in the wading pool. Only now my best friends were sea lions. And they seemed to be smiling at me as if they enjoyed my company.

I bobbed up out of the water to catch my breath, filled with emotions I couldn't describe. I wiped the hair from my face and saw Ron standing in the distance beyond the tank. He was leaning on the handle of the black umbrella, laughing. "How does it feel?" he asked.

"Fantastic!" I shouted.

As I rubbed my eyes, a shaft of sunlight emerged from the clouds and filtered down behind Ron, silhouetting his figure against the sky. As I stared at him, I came to an awesome realization. I loved Cameron Cavendish. I loved him with a capital *L*. He was my white knight, perfect from the top of his head of wavy brown hair to the tips of his toes. I'd climb a mountain, swim an ocean, or walk barefoot over hot coals for him.

To my surprise, that made me feel terribly uncomfortable.

I was dripping wet as I sat next to Ron in the cab coming home. The whole experience had left me totally speechless. The driver pulled up at my doorstep, Ron opened the door, and I got out in silence.

"Are you okay?" Ron asked, walking me into the lobby. "You're so quiet—is everything all right?"

"Oh yes," I said softly. "Everything is wonderful. I'll never forget this morning. It's the most marvelous thing that ever happened to me. How'd you get the zookeeper to agree to it?"

"That's my secret," he said, kissing me.

"You must've bribed him. Did it cost a lot? How'd you come up with such a great idea? What made you think of it?"

"It just came to me," he said, kissing me again. "Maybe because I needed to stay in your good graces because I've got to break our date for Tuesday."

"So do I," I told him. "I'm busy that night."

"Doing what?"

"Making money."

"I missed you yesterday," he said. "I wanted to see you but my mother had a million things for me to do."

He nibbled my ear. "You smell of fish."

"Why didn't you get in the tank with me? God, it was a great feeling! I can't believe this all really happened."

"Don't tell your friends—they'll all want fantasies fulfilled."

"Can you come upstairs?" I asked him.

"Nope. I've got to be someplace."

"You're the most wonderful person I've ever met," I told him. Then I kissed him. "You're absolutely marvelous, Cameron Cavendish."

Ron stared at me with a disturbed expression.

"Listen, there's something I wanted to say almost since we met. Something I should've told you."

"What is it?" I asked. Suddenly the cab driver honked and Ron was distracted. "Well? What?"

Ron kissed me again then said, "You're absolutely marvelous too, Molly Malone. That's what. See you."

I waved as he got back into the cab.

I sniffed my T-shirt. It did reek of fish. I hoped it would smell that way forever!

# Fourteen

They say love does strange things to people. Me it turned into an amoeba! For the next twenty-four hours I was a quivering mass of spongy jelly. I couldn't work or eat or anything. All I could focus on was Ron and my thrilling experience in the sea lion tank.

Mom was in her own world, so she didn't notice mine had irrevocably changed. Her plan to go back into show business had suddenly become definite, and she spent every spare minute ransacking the house searching for her old music sheets. "Pretty soon it'll be no more listening to Chopin sonatinas plucked out by sticky little fingers," she said intensely. I swear, she looked demented! She wandered around emptying drawers, dumping out boxes, and scattering debris around, like Ophelia scattering flowers. "I hope you haven't torn up my music," she said with concern.

I could barely hear her. Ron had pushed buttons in me I didn't know existed. Suddenly I was thinking about sappy things like whether or not he liked my hair or if I should switch deodorants—junk I never worried about with Isaac.

All afternoon I sat listening to Mendelssohn's Violin Concerto in E Minor. Now it was our song. During the *Allegro molto appassionato*, I imagined Ron and me waltzing around an ornate Victorian ballroom. Ron was leading me with breathtaking speed, and I was dancing better than Ann Reinking ever could. With the *Andante*, we were swimming in the sea lion tank, darting about in a thrilling chase that was followed by passionate underwater embraces.

I stared up at the ceiling and sighed.

Mom stood in the doorway clutching some yellowed music sheets. "Did you use it?" she asked.

"Use what?"

"My Cole Porter music. I only found some of it. Did you tear it up for a collage?"

"A collage?" I asked stupidly. The word sounded strangely foreign and unfamiliar.

"Well—did you take it or didn't you?" Mom asked.

"Take what?"

Mom looked exasperated. "What's wrong with you today? Can't you remember if you put it in a collage?"

"I guess I can't," I admitted.

I could barely remember my *name*.

Enough of that—Cameron Cavendish aside, I had

a life! Moping around being lovesick all day wasn't productive. Feeling passionately romantic wasn't overly terrific, either. I took a long cold shower and pulled myself together.

On Tuesday the dinner at the Metropolitan Museum was scheduled to begin with cocktails at six, so Leonard told me to arrive at four. We had two hours setting-up time.

It felt strange not paying my usual penny at the entrance and getting my MMA button. I told the guard I was waitressing the party that night.

"Which one?" he asked.

"Which? Why, how many have you got?"

He took out a piece of paper. "We've got a party for a new perfume in the Englehard Court. We've got a wedding reception in the Temple of Dendur, and we've got a charity benefit in the Medieval Sculpture Hall."

"No kidding? The joint is really jumping."

"Yeah, it's a triple-header."

"Doesn't that get confusing?"

"Sure does," he said, chuckling at the thought. "Sometimes cocktails are in one place, and dinner is in another. Sometimes it gets to look like they're moving cattle around a feedlot in here! That's why parties have to run on schedule, just like clockwork."

"I'm going to the Medieval Sculpture Hall," I told him.

"Okay, those galleries have already been closed off."

131

"Really? What if someone flies in from Cleveland longing to grab a quick look at relics or something?"

The guard shrugged. "I guess he's out of luck."

"I guess." I noticed this guard had a much chummier attitude than I usually get from these guys. When I'm a visitor, the guards ignore my role in the passing human parade because their eyes are too busy riveting onto the button that verifies I paid admission. But now we were both employees—both buttonless, on equal footing—and the Met was our boss. "Three parties at a fee of thirty thousand dollars a shot? Not bad for one night," I said.

"Not bad," he agreed.

"Well, so long. Don't take any wooden buttons."

Even though some galleries had already been closed off in preparation for the parties, there were still crowds in the museum. I guess they were unaware that the nouveaux riches would soon be running amok through the halls.

I gave my name to the guard near the entrance to the Sculpture Hall. He checked it off a list, then pointed me toward the side stairway. As I went down the steps, I noticed crates of Dom Perignon stacked along the floor.

Leonard had explained to me that all the cooking is actually done in advance so heating up is all that's required. Even so, everyone looked awfully busy. Several people were setting up the temporary kitchen in the halls, while others unpacked chafing dishes and butane pots.

A thin, harried-looking young woman with straight

blond hair seemed to be in charge so I went over to introduce myself. "Are you Nancy, the caterer?" I asked. She nodded yes. "Hi, I'm Molly, one of your waitresses for tonight."

Nancy squeezed out from behind a microwave being placed on a portable cart. "I hope you're good," she said nervously. "Leonard swore you had experience. Is that right?"

"Not with private parties," I admitted. "But I've waitressed a lot in restaurants."

"That's good, because this bash tonight is a real killer. Platter service, six courses. And special uniforms, too. Once the party rental people set up the chairs and tables, you can begin the place settings, okay?"

"Sure."

Nancy checked each utensil off her list, then maneuvered her way around a rack of serving platters. "Excuse me, I've got to check in with the florist. He just forced open two thousand white irises, and now he's worried the steam from my suckling pig will make them wither before dessert."

"Suckling pig?" I asked, noticing Leonard arriving.

"Right," said Nancy, hurrying away. "Lenny will fill you in."

"Is she really serving suckling pig?" I asked. "How positively medieval."

"That's the idea," said Leonard. "Trust the rich to outdo one another. Our host decided to re-create a baronial meal from the fourteenth century, so he insisted Nancy stick to a menu from an early cookbook. This dinner was served to Richard II, can you believe it? Nancy had to hire a food researcher before she could start."

"I didn't know they had Dom Perignon in the Middle Ages," I observed.

"I guess Nancy made some tiny concessions to modernity," said Leonard. "Hell, the guests need something to wash down their sweetmeats."

"Where'd you learn all this?"

"I read the society columns. It's my only vice."

"So tell me, who is throwing this party?"

"One of the super-rich in search of a fun charity. This bash is to raise money for some endangered species. It'll be wall-to-wall limos outside this joint in a couple of hours."

As I helped Leonard unpack the dishes, I noticed the peculiar pleasure he got from the entire deal.

"I did my own research into the Middle Ages," he told me. "Did you know that after a meal was finished, pieces of gravy-soaked bread were distributed to the poor, along with the scraps? Do you think they'll do that tonight? . . . Nah, maybe they'll let *us* eat them."

"How come you're getting such a kick out of all this?" I asked.

"I love irony," he said dramatically.

"Me, too," I said, "so lead me to the spits, mortars, and pestles."

"Sorry, we'll have to make do with aluminum trays and sterno."

"Have you got a rundown of the menu?"

Leonard looked like the proverbial cat who had just swallowed the canary. "I thought you'd never ask.

There's clove-and-raisin wine for starters. For non-boozers, there's mulled cider. We begin with chicken broth and finish with raspberries and cream, pears with spun sugar. In between there's poached fish with saffron and honey. Later, roast rabbit, suckling pig, a boar's head garnished with fresh flowers, venison, woodcock, and pheasant."

"You're joking! Where's the fatted calf? Why not throw in some peacock tongues?" My initial disgust turned to delight when I realized *I* would be the recipient of the garbage from the world's most decadent meal. What a great social statement I could make! Happily, I began piling dishes onto trays.

"Don't forget those finger bowls," someone shouted at me.

"Yes, people were very fussy in the fourteenth century," Leonard noted.

Nancy returned wheeling a cart piled high with large covered aluminum trays. "You'd better start getting into your costume," she told me.

"What costume?"

"Didn't Leonard tell you? You'll dress as medieval servants. The men will say 'M'lord' and the gals say 'I'm your serving wench.' "

I didn't believe it. "You made that up."

Another waitress passed me and smiled. "Relax, there's a hundred bucks extra for everyone who says it."

"But that's demeaning," I protested. "Besides, who'll know if we say it or not?"

"Beats me, honey," she told me. "So don't say it.

Me, I don't mind. I'm a serving wench at home for nothing. Here, I tell it like it is and make an extra hundred."

"I can't wait to see this costume," I groaned.

My serving wench outfit was hanging in the bathroom. It was a long black taffeta skirt and a low-cut blouse that laced up the middle and had short puffy sleeves. When I put it on, I had to admit it looked awfully cute. And sexy, too. I began to get into the feel of things. Okay, so I'd be a serving wench, what the hell!

When I returned, Nancy was lighting the butane pots. She and her three assistants were heating up the large aluminum food trays. "You look real good," she told me.

As I carried a trayful of wine glasses into the Sculpture Hall, wonderful aromas began wafting through the corridors. Beyond the gates of the Medieval Court, they were putting the finishing touches on the decor. Dozens of round tables and folding chairs had been draped with bright brocades and velvets. In the center of each table stood an arrangement of white irises.

It seemed strange to see modern dinner tables scattered between the medieval art and sacred objects. The glass display cases contained sculptures of religious subjects—marbles of monks, saints, and virgin martyrs, and wooden statues of Christ's crucifixion, penitents in sorrow and flagellation.

If the dinner tables looked incongruous, the art did, too. The medieval period was a strange combination of religion and chivalry; people's obsession with the cult

136

of ideal love was almost as great as their obsession with the Church. Flemish tapestries depicting the landed gentry engaged in falconry and revelry hung across the stone walls above the antique oak choir stalls.

Leonard followed behind me with a trayful of glasses. "They had a real warped mind-set in those days," he noted. "This age of castles and chivalry was also the age of St. Francis. Do you know what happened to the followers of Francis who shared his vow of poverty? After he died, they were all burned at the stake as heretics. See, by then, the Church was heavily into banking and didn't approve of that poverty stuff. It was much too subversive."

In the corners of the Sculpture Hall, canopies had been erected and draped in silky fabrics. Beneath the draperies, a lutist, a hurdy-gurdy minstrel, and a harpist were tuning up. The minstrel had a variety of Renaissance instruments with him, including flutes and pipes. I recognized the harpist from the Seventy-seventh Street flea market. She was a street performer who played there on Sundays. They were all dressed in medieval outfits.

A tall thin man wearing gauzy white slacks and looking flustered rushed back and forth supervising everything. The interior designer for this shindig, no doubt.

Leonard started setting out the china and silverware. "Have you decided yet?" he asked. "Are you going to be their serving wench tonight?"

"Sure, why not? It's sexist but the dinner's for charity so I guess I don't mind."

137

Leonard grinned. "Someday I'd love to discuss the intricate process you've devised in order to make your monetary and moral decisions."

He glanced at my outfit. "Sexist perhaps, but also very sexy. Don't let the lord of the manor take advantage. Actually, in medieval days, bedding privileges came with the territory. That's one thing the rich have to pay for now."

Then Leonard modeled his costume for me: black tights and a long white shirt tied at the hips. "You like it?"

"Yes, you're pretty sexy, too," I told him. "I've never seen a waiter in tights before."

As we set the tables, I kept thinking Leonard was enjoying some private joke. "Does waitering turn you on or what? I've never seen you so jolly."

He smiled as he showed me how to fold the linen napkins into rosettes. "Maybe you're used to seeing me as Rempha, but he's only a character. Rempha is above the human comedy, Molly; Leonard is very much a part of it. Or maybe I like serving my betters. Maybe watching the overprivileged enjoy their privileges turns me on."

"Maybe you're right," I agreed. "So far I'm enjoying this whole deal."

"Wait until six o'clock. When the nouveaux riches and the glitterati reach critical mass, you'll change your mind!"

By quarter to six, Nancy had everything under control. I was impressed at how efficiently she assembled her precooked gourmet meal inside the makeshift temporary kitchen. "Is there really a boar's head lurking under one of those lids?" I asked.

"Not a real one," she explained. "It's mainly for effect—we didn't think anyone would want to eat it, so I made one with dough." She lifted the foil cover on the oval platter to reveal a beautifully shaped boar's head, glazed to perfection.

"You're quite an artist," I told her.

"Anything for money," she said. "What's this about you wanting my garbage? Leonard mentioned something, but it didn't make sense. Why do you want pheasant and rabbit bones?"

"Detritus for my artwork," I explained. "Can I have a copy of the menu and the champagne labels, too?"

"Whatever turns you on," said Nancy. "When this job's over I'm out of here and home to my cheese sandwich."

As six o'clock approached, I lined up with the other waitresses to take out hors d'oeuvres while the waiters gathered up the drink trays.

Leonard balanced a trayful of wine glasses in each hand. "The lords and ladies hath arrived," he announced.

"Okay everyone, get out there," said Nancy. "Pass the hors d'oeuvres and make sure everyone has something to drink."

"Right," said Leonard. "Check them out, the overdressed and the underweight, the Junior Leaguers and the Bush Leaguers. No radicals, liberals, or individuals—just moguls and magnates. But watch out for the girls with prematurely large hair—it's a contagious disease they inherited from their mothers." He nudged me toward the steps. "Climb those stairs and discover the future that awaits you. Learn the whole world is Republican, and it's going to the Hamptons."

"Quit clowning and move your ass!" Nancy ordered.

As Leonard and I hurried up the stairs we could hear the harp and lute music echoing through the Sculpture Hall. "I'm sure seeing a different side of you tonight," I told him.

"I bet you'll see lots of things tonight," he replied. Then he disappeared into the crowd of gathering guests.

# Fifteen

A re you ever surprised at how closely fiction mirrors reality? I mean, life typecasts people just like movies do. I thought of that when I first saw the host and hostess for tonight's party. They were standing inside the wrought-iron gates of the Medieval Court, greeting their guests as they arrived. Mrs. Hostess wore a glittering swirl of lemon-yellow satin. Glistening cabochon emeralds hung from her dainty pink earlobes and across her white throat. She had large dark eyes and her black hair was pulled back severely. Every inch of this woman spelled class. She had what artists call a *retroussé* nose—long, then upturned in a very regal manner. Sargent would have loved to paint her.

Her husband, Mr. Host, was no slouch either. He

was tall, gray-haired, and distinguished—also from the silver-spoon school.

As the guests started to arrive, Harlequin-costumed acrobats on stilts, serenading minstrels, and jugglers strolled among them. The hurdy-gurdy man and the harpist played, and the guy with the lute sang English madrigals. And we, the peasant folk, busied ourselves serving our lords and ladies. Life hadn't changed much in five hundred years!

I didn't make a terrific waitress. I got so caught up watching people arrive, I kept forgetting to serve them.

"Keep circulating," said Leonard, nudging me.

I continued passing the hors d'oeuvres. I tried to be unobtrusive, but I couldn't help eavesdropping on people's conversations. The guests were everything Leonard said they'd be: upper-echelon society elite.

"You cannot teach a person flower arranging," said one woman. "It is an instinct in the genes."

"She hasn't a brain in her head," another woman sadly noted to a friend. "It's a pathetically tragic relationship."

"Isn't it nice to be civilized again?" said a man. He had gray, slicked-back hair and a white waxy mustache. "I'm so relieved this is a good charity." He spent a long time analyzing my hors d'oeuvres, then refused them all.

An old woman with a hawk nose commented, "Sometimes I feel there is too much of everything everywhere."

"*Oui*," said her companion.

The younger people hung out together in a separate corner. As they arrived, the girls would squeal with

142

delight and air-kiss each other, then admire one another's de la Rentas and Bill Blasses, bought especially for the occasion.

By now I was in the swing of things, too. I smiled and said, "Hi, I'm your serving wench," to everyone as I passed the goodies.

Then I noticed a girl propel herself across the room, her long blond hair flying. She was wearing a strapless magenta satin gown that showed off her tan beautifully.

I recognized her at once. It was Francie-poo from Central Park.

In that split second as I stared at her, her entire life flashed before my eyes. She'd been born to become the Deb of the Year, the Hour, or the Minute!

She stared at me, too. To her, I was a displaced person. Where had she seen me before? It was that look you give grocery clerks and bank tellers when you see them on the street, out from behind their counters and away from familiar surroundings.

I wondered how Ron had gotten chummy with a girl like this. Did she know Ron's mother's employers, the Spratts?

"Hi, I'm your serving wench," I told her, offering her an hors d'oeuvre.

Francie-poo refused. She was too busy greeting the other guests, who all seemed overjoyed to see her. Francie-poo was very popular.

The host and hostess approached. "Francine, I was afraid you weren't coming," said Mrs. Host.

"Good evening, Mrs. Spratt," she replied.

*Mrs. Spratt?* I nearly dropped my hors d'oeuvre tray.

143

Nancy gestured from the corner. It was time to start serving the first course. I hurried down the stairs and began piling the soup bowls onto trays. Leonard, who was a whiz at it, was way ahead of me.

"What a coincidence," I told him. "The hosts for this party are Mr. and Mrs. Worthington Spratt."

He didn't seem surprised. "The *Second*," he added. "Never forget that part, Molly. Worthington Spratt the Second. It forms a symmetry with Richard the Second, the originator of this feast."

"Why didn't you tell me?" I asked. "Didn't you know Ron's mother works for them as a house-keeper?"

"You don't say. . . . Small world. Like I said, you'll learn lots of things tonight."

I didn't like the way he said that.

When I returned to the party, the beeswax candles at each table had been lit, and a waiter was draping a chain of fresh flowers around the display platter of phony wild boar.

Francie-poo was seated at the main table next to Mrs. Spratt. I figured she must be a good friend of the family. She threw me a glance. "Those waitress outfits are the greatest, Mrs. Spratt. Wherever did you get the idea?"

"Lydia wanted everything authentic," explained Mr. Spratt. "But I told her if that were the case, we'd have sawdust on the floor and dozens of dogs wandering around the place. I explained she'd have to make concessions, and she agreed—but she insisted on the costumes."

Mrs. Spratt stroked her husband's hand. "We can't

144

feel medieval with the waiters wearing tuxedoes—can we, my love?"

Francine didn't bother listening to the explanation. She was too busy craning her neck, checking out the other guests.

"Hi, I'm your serving wench," I said as I placed a porcelain bowl of broth in front of her.

"Francine, who are you searching for?" asked Mrs. Spratt.

"I'm looking for my date, of course. I know he's always shamefully late, but this is inexcusable."

Mr. Spratt laughed. "Face it, that boy won't be on time for his own funeral."

"It's not chic to be late to benefits," scolded Mrs. Spratt, "especially *mine*."

"Hi, I'm your serving wench," I said as I placed a bowl of broth in front of Mr. Spratt.

Mr. Spratt turned to me with a look of annoyance. "Lydia, does this poor girl have to repeat that every time she makes a move?"

Mrs. Spratt smiled at me. It was the typically benevolent smile of someone accustomed to dealing with underlings. "Perhaps you should use your own discretion," she advised.

What'd *that* mean? Should I say "Yes, ma'am" or curtsey or what? I put down the next bowl without saying anything, but I started to feel ill at ease. I felt badly prepared for my servile role, but I consoled myself with the thought of the glorious garbage that would soon await me.

Leonard and I bumped into each other in the corridor.

"How's it going?" he asked.

"Okay, but maybe we could switch tables? It makes me nervous to serve the Spratts."

"Sorry, a good waiter never switches. The host would think it's odd. Besides, I arranged for you to have the head table. So you see, Molly, the die is cast. You've got to take this to its inevitable conclusion, only don't say I didn't warn you."

I was getting sick of Leonard's sarcastic comments. "What's your problem tonight? Huh?"

He stared at me—a little malevolently, I thought. "You'd better hurry back up with the fish," he said.

When I returned, Francie-poo's date had finally arrived.

I blinked several times as I watched him standing by the table.

*It was Ron.*

Cameron Cavendish had broken his date with me to accompany Francie-poo to this benefit bash.

Ron didn't notice me at first. He was too busy making kissyface with Francie. If he had seen me, he wouldn't have recognized me anyway. People rarely notice other people who have suddenly turned into servants.

I was livid. How dare he break his date with me, then turn around and date someone else? What kind of creep was he, anyhow?

I felt like running to find someplace to hide. Instead, I marched over to the Spratt table and placed the dish of poached fish in front of Ron. "Hi, I'm your serving wench," I said with a saccharine tone, "and how are you this evening?"

146

Ron's mouth fell open. "*Molly?* What are *you* doing here?"

"I'm your serving wench," I repeated, "that's what."

Francie-poo gave me a closer look. "Isn't this the girl you were with in Central Park?"

Mrs. Spratt looked confused. "Cameron, do you know this young lady?"

Ron looked embarrassed. He didn't say anything.

Mr. Spratt sensed something was peculiar. "Cameron, please answer your mother." Then he looked at me. "Please excuse my son's rudeness."

I couldn't believe what he'd said. "*Your son?*" I asked. I stared at Ron. "I thought you were Mrs. C.'s son. You said your name was Cameron Cavendish."

"I never told you that," Ron insisted.

"How confusing," said Mrs. Spratt, growing uncomfortable. Years of hostessing and all her impeccable party etiquette hadn't prepared her for this particular moment. She stared at me, then asked, "Would you please serve the fish?"

I served the fish. I felt like throwing it at someone, but I served it. Then I returned to Ron's seat. "Why did you lie to me?" I asked under my breath.

"I never lied to you," he whispered.

"You've lied since the minute we met," I said angrily, my voice getting louder.

Ron started getting hot under the collar. "This isn't the place to discuss it," he argued.

Francie-poo was getting annoyed, too. "Ron, since you two seem to be such good friends, perhaps you should introduce us."

"Sure," he said, "this is Molly Malone."

"Really?" she asked.

"Yes. Why? Have you heard of me?"

She stared at me blankly. "No. Should I have?" She kept staring. "Oh. Do you mean that old song?"

I was feeling awfully stupid.

Mrs. Spratt managed a weak smile. "It's nice to meet you, Molly." Then a glazed expression crossed her face. Had she been too familiar? Would I consider it an invitation to *sit down at their table?* She needn't have worried—I wouldn't dream of it!

"I didn't know Molly would be here tonight," said Ron.

"Obviously," said Francie-poo sarcastically.

Everyone looked uncomfortable, but I didn't move. I couldn't. I guess I was waiting for an explanation. I wanted Ron to tell me why he'd broken our date and why he had pretended to be the son of a housekeeper when he was actually the son of Worthington Spratt II, some big-deal society millionaire.

"The fish is superb," said Mr. Spratt.

"Thank you," said Mrs. Spratt, as if she'd caught and poached the thing herself.

"Excuse me, I'll be right back," I told them.

But I didn't go back.

When I got downstairs, I ran into the bathroom and changed into my own clothes.

Then I tore out of the Metropolitan Museum of Art without looking back.

# Sixteen

≈≈≈

I cried all night.
Why had Ron lied to me? Was it his idea of a joke or what?

I didn't think it was funny.

The next morning I went to the library to find out all I could about the Spratt family. I dragged out old listings of society's Four Hundred in the Social Register, *Who's Who*, and tons of press clippings.

Worthington Spratt II was old money that went back several generations. His grandfather had started the Spratt Foundation, whose favorite charities were the New York Zoological Society and the New York Public Library. Mr. Spratt was the CEO of a major investment firm. He and his wife, Lydia, spent most of their time hopping back and forth from Palm Beach to Fifth Avenue to the Hamptons.

Lydia Spratt was in the thick of society's War of the Hostesses race, trying to see who could chair the most benefits. She was on the board of the Metropolitan Opera, the New York Philharmonic, and the Metropolitan Museum. Animals were her favorite cause, and her annual Pet Fete, one of society's hottest tickets, raised millions for the Bronx and Central Park zoos.

Ha! No wonder it was so easy for Ron to get me in to feed the sea lions.

I did some reading up on Ron, too. I checked through some back issues of the *New York Times* society page, where he was mentioned more than once. Last summer he'd gone canoeing down the Orinoco River. On his spring break he'd gone on a penguin-banding expedition in Patagonia with the National Geographic Society.

What a jerk he must've thought I was, having fits over swimming with those damn sea lions!

I couldn't bear to read any more.

I felt used, humiliated, and idiotic.

I *hated* Cameron Spratt.

But to my great distress, I still cared about Cameron Cavendish.

The next day I moped around the house like a zombie. Ron telephoned me several times, but I refused to talk to him.

By that night, Mom was getting suspicious. "Why

150

won't you speak to this young man? He sounds very nice."

If Mom learned I was ignoring someone rich, she'd have forty fits. I couldn't risk her asking more questions, so I took the next call.

"What do you want?" I asked him.

"I want to see you, of course. I want to explain."

"I don't want to listen."

"You're the most stubborn person I ever met."

"And you're the most deceitful," I told him.

"I never lied to you, Molly. Not directly—and not intentionally. You drew some wrong conclusions, that's all. I should've straightened you out, but—well, I'll admit maybe it was fun having you think I was poor. People have always known I was rich, so I've never been sure how a girl would react to me if . . ."

"That's garbage. You know how I feel about that rich stuff."

"Hell yes, I found that out fast. But once we'd gotten to know each other I was already stuck with the lie. I never meant to hurt you. Can't we talk this out?"

I felt too confused. "I don't know," I said. "I don't think so. Not now, anyway. Maybe some other time. Listen, I've got to go."

I said good-bye, then hung up.

I was mad at Ron—and mad at myself, too.

The next day, I still had so many feelings I needed to vent that I went into my M.R. to work. I remembered the box of antique postcards Mrs. C. had given me. I dumped them out on the floor. I rummaged through the messages various Spratt relations had sent from the four corners of the earth. They were all signed with upright, upper-crust names like Sumner, Meredith, Wiley, and Aunt Penelope.

I was growing real tight inside. I had been mad at Ron for being deceitful, and now I was getting mad at all his ancestors. They all had traveled to places I'd probably never see, and somehow that made me furious!

I envisioned creating a collage, including the postcards and excerpts from the articles I'd read about Ron's family. Maybe I'd entitle it *Drat the Spratts!* What a pathetically petty idea, right? I pushed the cards aside. Then I cleared a space for the new project I'd already planned—my Prince George/Museum Dinner collage. But I suddenly realized I couldn't start that, either. I'd forfeited all my marvelous garbage when I ran out of the museum.

I'd left without the pheasant and rabbit bones, without the Dom Perignon labels and menus, without everything that would make my collage meaningful.

I stared at the wall for a while, beginning to recall lots of other things about that night. I threw on my clothes and decided to get over to the Metropolitan Museum. My garbage would be gone, but I had other unfinished business to attend to.

I wanted a few words with Leonard; he owed me an apology.

Look, I know creative artists aren't perfect, at least not in their personal lives. Picasso was an egotist, Beethoven was a crank, and Shakespeare wasn't nuts about his wife. But when an artist is doing his thing, he can create a perfect moment. And that's what Leonard does when he becomes Rempha.

When I arrived outside the Metropolitan, a large crowd was gathered beside the fountain to watch the mechanical man. You could hear a pin drop, they were so involved in Leonard's performance. I watched for fifteen minutes before he stopped, took a bow, and gathered up his donations while the crowd continued to applaud.

Despite how I felt about Leonard that moment, I was impressed. "That was inspired," I told him.

"Thanks," he said. He gently patted his brow, trying not to smear his gold makeup. I could tell he felt ill at ease. "Where have you been?" he asked. "I didn't see you at all yesterday. Nancy was angry. So I told her you left because you're a recovering alcoholic and you couldn't hang around the liquor. Nancy sympathizes with things like that."

"You shouldn't have lied for me. Besides, you know the real reason I ran out."

"Do I?" he asked, avoiding my glance.

"Why'd you do it, Leonard?"

"Do what?"

"You know what. You knew who Ron was, and you let me walk in there blind. It was a mean, rotten thing to do."

"Life can be mean sometimes, Molly. I thought you needed to know."

"Don't give me that. You could've told me yourself."

"I tried, but you wouldn't let me."

"You could have *told* me," I insisted. "Finding out that way made me feel like a fool."

Leonard adjusted his loudspeakers and changed the tape in his recorder. "I don't want to talk about it," he said flatly.

"Why'd you do it?" I shouted.

Leonard continued to avoid my glance as he inspected his battery pack. "Because all's fair in love and war, that's why."

"What kind of comment is that? Which one is this supposed to be?"

A sad expression crossed his face. "It's the former, Molly—unfortunately. As it turns out, very unfortunately for me."

"Let's quit the sarcasm, okay?" I yelled. "What you did the other night was mean and shitty, and I need to know why."

"I told you—because I love you, that's why. And because I think it's mean and shitty that you never noticed that fact."

I stared at him. He wasn't joking, he was serious. I gulped. "You can't love me," I said. "I mean, we've never even . . ."

"Even what?" he asked, confronting me. "Tell me, what? Haven't we spent hours talking about life, our goals, our beliefs, dozens of different things? Don't we have all kinds of stuff in common? Well, don't we? We share opinions on books and artists, right? We even like the same dumb Doowop songs. So what haven't we done together, Molly? We haven't slept together, that's all."

154

"I haven't slept with Ron, either," I admitted.

Leonard shook his head. "But you think you love him, right? C'mon, *we've* shared lots more stuff together."

"Maybe we have, but it's not the same."

"No. At least you know Spratt's last name now—his real one, I mean. You never asked me mine." As Leonard turned away, a pathetic whine entered his voice. "You never even *asked* me my last name, damn it!"

I stared at his back, speechless. He was right, I didn't know his last name—and until he'd mentioned it, I hadn't known I didn't know it. It was true, we'd spent lots of time together, sharing opinions, arguing, asking and giving each other advice. God, I felt terrible.

"I'm sorry," I said feebly, "I never—hey, how was I supposed to know the way you felt?"

He didn't answer.

"Now I'm all mixed up," I said. "I came to chew you out but—well, how was I supposed to know?"

"Don't lose sleep over it," he finally said. "After this weekend I may be out of here, anyway. That gig in Florida is still open, so I think I'll take it. If it works out, I can be their permanent Mickey Mouse—as long as I stay humble. They tell me their former rodent got swellheaded and couldn't fit into the costume."

"You mean you wouldn't come back to New York?"

"Maybe not." Leonard removed a Ziplock bag from a satchel tucked underneath his tape deck and handed it to me.

"Rabbit bones and pheasant feathers. I saved them."

155

"That was thoughtful."

He shrugged. "I'm glad to get them off my hands, they're stinking up my satchel. Here's a menu, too. And some champagne labels. I took the bottles home and steamed them off for you."

"Hey, thanks a lot. I appreciate it."

"You're the only girl who would." Leonard glanced toward the fountain. A sizable crowd was waiting for him to return. "Excuse me, my public awaits."

"Things won't be the same around here without you," I told him. "Ever since I started selling, you've been here, too."

Leonard stared at the pavement. "All of life is change—or so they say."

"By the way, what is it? Your last name, I mean."

"Pressman."

"So long, Leonard Pressman."

"So long, Molly Malone."

I wanted to hug him, but I was afraid I'd smear his gold makeup.

I walked home through Central Park. I didn't have my hand truck or any of the selling equipment I usually took, but I felt weighted down, anyway.

My mind was a confused mess. Leonard Pressman loved me. All these months I'd never known his last name, he'd loved me. Had he fantasized about us? In his imagination, had we danced the waltz together? Sailed down placid Venetian canals? Made love underwater?

Why didn't I love him back? If ever two people were

psychologically suited, it was probably the two of us. So why had I fallen for Ron instead? Did it all come down to chemistry? Was one of life's most meaningful experiences based on nothing but a chemical equation?

A strange lethargy overtook me, and I sensed an overwhelming numbness flood my body, as if someone had poured molten lead into every pore. I attributed it to the heat. And I was grateful for it.

# Seventeen

I missed my kids. When I was with them I forgot everything else. I decided our art lesson that evening would consist of making things from balsa wood. The boys had been grumbling about too much sissy stuff lately, and I knew they'd enjoy constructing airplanes and guns instead. I didn't want the lack of pretty colors to dissuade Sonja, so I planned to show her how to cut out flowers from the thin wooden sheets.

As it turned out, Sonja wasn't waiting for me when I arrived at the hotel. The lobby was steaming hot, and the kids who'd shown up looked unusually sluggish. Mitchell was even more withdrawn than usual, and everyone else seemed surly, too. Antoine was acting up, and Monty was itching for a fight. No one seemed interested in the art project. Was it the awful heat? I wondered.

I went to the desk clerk. "Don't you have some fans you could turn on? It's like an oven in here."

He looked up from his magazine and stared at me blankly. "It's even hotter upstairs," he said, as if that made everything okay. Then he returned to reading.

Monty had begun horsing around, smacking Darryl real hard over the head with a balsa wood packet.

"What's up with you?" I asked, grabbing it away from him. "How come you guys are acting so lousy? And where's Sonja? Is something wrong around here?"

In a fit of anger, Monty grabbed the package from me and hurled it across the lobby. "What's it your damn business?" he shouted. Then he pushed me aside and hurried to the elevator.

I ran after him and grabbed his shoulder. "What's wrong?" I asked.

He pulled away. "Hey, man, lots of things are wrong, okay? This ain't no Beverly Hills hotel, ya know."

"Sure I know. So tell me what's up."

"Uh-uh, I gotta go," he protested.

"Are all you kids okay? Where's Sonja? Why didn't she come down tonight?"

"Forget it," he said angrily. "Sonja won't be comin' down no more."

"How come?" I asked.

Monty turned his face away. "Sonja stays in her room now," he explained.

"Why?"

"She just does, okay."

I couldn't get a straight answer! "How come? Is she sick?" Monty still refused to look at me. He shifted his weight from one foot to the other. "How come?" I asked insistently.

His voice began to quiver. "The other night, a couple guys got crazy on crack. They seen Sonja running around, and they messed with her, man."

I wasn't sure what he meant. "Do you mean they attacked her? Was she molested?"

Monty stared at me, his eyes filled with pain. "Yeah, they messed with her real bad. Do I gotta spell it out for you? Anyway, now she don't talk to no one no more, not even me."

I couldn't believe it—at least, I didn't want to. "What did the police do?" I asked. "Did Sonja's mother report it? Did she notify the social welfare agencies?"

Monty sneered. "Get real, okay. Ain't nobody gonna do somethin' about it. Worse stuff happens here every day. Everything goes down in here, and ain't nobody gives a shit."

"I'm sorry," I said weakly. "I don't know what else to say."

Monty pounded his fists against the wall. "Bastards," he shouted, "filthy bastards!" He kept pounding until his knuckles were raw.

Finally I grabbed Monty's hands away and pulled him toward me. I wanted to hug him but he pushed me away. "Listen," I said, "I know how awful you must feel. Maybe it'd help to talk about it?" Fighting back tears, he shook his head. "Is there anything I can do?" He shook his head again. "Are you sure?"

160

"I gotta go now, man," he insisted.

"Okay, but maybe you'll want to talk later." I wrote down my phone number and gave it to him. "You can talk to me about anything—anytime—understand? I don't care when it is, okay?"

Monty didn't reply, but he put the paper in his pocket. Then he got into the elevator.

I spent the next day on the telephone, trying to get help for Sonja. I called every agency I could find in the phone book. Each one put me off, put me on hold, switched me to another line or recommended another agency. Or else they generally ignored me.

Instead of answering questions, they asked me: "What's your interest in this case?"

"Are you a relative?"

"Are you a resident of the Prince George?"

"What's your Social Security number?"

"What's your Medicaid number?"

Or else they'd tell me: "Sorry, we have no information regarding those services."

"Sorry, you'll have to speak to the supervisor."

"Sorry, he's not here right now."

Sorry, sorry, sorry.

But I refused to give up. Finally (either by accident or fate) I was put in touch with someone who knew something. Ironically, Mr. Morales didn't work for a city agency. He ran a small shelter/soup kitchen in a local church near the Prince George, and he knew a lot about cutting through red tape. "What's the problem?" he asked when I called.

I explained the problem. Then I told him that Sonja's mother probably never reported the attack. Mr. Morales said it probably wouldn't have done much good if she had.

"Maybe so," I said, "but I want to make sure Sonja receives some kind of help—whatever she'll need."

"I'll check into it," Mr. Morales said. "The city is trying to phase families out of that welfare hotel. Hell, kids don't belong in a place like that."

"No one does," I said. "Even jails allow visitors. I'd like to see Sonja and her mother, but the rules forbid it. I can't go upstairs. Isn't that crazy?"

"How old is the girl?" Mr. Morales asked.

"Six. Almost seven."

I could hear him sigh. "Hell, that's awful. Okay, maybe I can arrange for her to get some counseling or therapy. I'll make a few phone calls and see what I can do. Check back with me."

I thanked him and hung up. At last I felt I might have accomplished something.

That night, Ron called. "Remember me? We've got a lot to talk about. When can I see you? I've been trying to get through to you all day."

"I've been on the phone all day," I explained. "Something awful happened to Sonja, one of my kids at the Prince George. She was molested."

"That's terrible. I'm sorry, Molly. Do you want to talk about it?"

"No, I've been talking about it for hours. That's why this phone has been so busy. I've been trying to arrange some help for Sonja."

"I see," said Ron. "Well, then this obviously isn't the right time to talk about us, either."

"Wait, maybe it is. After all, we've got things to settle. We'd better meet."

We met in Angela's Coffee Shop on Broadway. As we sat staring into our cups, I wondered if this would be the place I'd tell Ron off, too—as I had Isaac before him. There'd be symmetry in that. But I didn't want to tell him off. I wanted answers. "I was real angry when I saw you at the benefit with Francie-poo," I admitted.

"But Francine and I grew up together. We went to the same school."

"*Private* school, no doubt."

"That's right, private school. Francine is like a sister to me. There's no reason for you to be jealous of her."

"I didn't say I was jealous. I said I was angry. Why'd you break our date to take her to the benefit?"

"Francine is a junior member of one of Mother's committees," Ron explained.

"I read all about your mother in the library," I told him. "I read up on your whole family and all the charities they're involved in. They say Mrs. Worthington Spratt's Pet Fete is quite a hot ticket. You're a positive social wallflower if you don't attend."

Ron ignored my sarcasm. "Mother raises a lot of money for endangered species."

"Yeah, well, I guess it's real chic to give to charities like that, isn't it? But if you ask me, being socially conscious means more than going to black-tie dinners.

163

Not that Francie the Deb-of-the-Minute would agree. I'll bet she was cloned to attend parties. I'll bet she's had that smile of hers permanently grafted on her face."

"Yes, Francine knows how to be charming," Ron agreed.

"And I don't, I suppose? Sorry, maybe that's something you can only learn in expensive private schools."

"Look, Molly, I didn't ask Francine to that benefit. Mother arranged the whole thing weeks ago without ever consulting me."

"My, my, I'll bet you have a very active social calendar." I could hear I was getting nastier every second, but I couldn't stop myself.

Ron was getting angry. "You act as if I'm a leper, just because you discovered I'm rich."

"And you act like I'm not good enough to take to a fancy benefit," I shouted. "It must've been a laugh riot watching me swim around in that sea lion tank. Francie-poo must've split a gut when you told her about it."

"You looked great in that tank," Ron said. "You looked beautiful. What's this really about, Molly? My taking Francine to a party or my being rich? Knock the chip off and tell me what you're really angry about. Why are you making such an incredible deal of this?"

I wasn't sure why. Did I feel inferior? Did I want a white knight who was absolutely perfect? Was I *afraid* to love Ron? Maybe I was looking for an excuse not to even like him. "I don't know who you are," I said. "I thought I did, but I don't. I knew someone named Cameron Cavendish—not Spratt."

164

"Fair enough," Ron said. "Maybe that means we should start over again."

"Maybe," I said haltingly.

"Shall I apologize again?" he asked. "I wanted to tell you who I was that night in the theater, but we had no time together. Afterward, you hit me with that speech about lousy rich people, which put me off. Look, I'm not excusing myself but—well, if you didn't have such strong opinions about everything, maybe . . ."

"Great, so now it's my fault, right?"

Ron pushed his chair from the table. "Look, I'd like to patch up this relationship before I leave, but . . ."

"Hold it," I said, "I wasn't sure you thought this was a relationship. And where are you going, anyway?"

"My parents have a place in the Hamptons. We're spending the month there." The waitress passed, and Ron asked for more coffee. "I don't want to leave before we've straightened things out. Can't we start over again?"

"How big is this place in the Hamptons?" I asked.

"Ten rooms."

"With an enormous pool, I suppose?"

"That's right," Ron said. "Is that relevant?"

"I don't know," I confessed. "I'm real mixed up. I keep seeing you and Francie-darling laughing your heads off over me. That business with the Danish— did you tell her about that, too? And ushering? Damn, why didn't you let me know Mrs. C. wasn't your mother? What a rotten lie that was!"

"I didn't lie," Ron argued. "Okay, technically maybe I did. I let you believe something that wasn't true. But I've never mentioned you to Francine. Why should I?"

"That's right, why should you?"

Ron was getting impatient. He tapped his finger on the rim of his cup and didn't say anything for a long time.

"Well, what are you thinking?" I finally asked.

"I'm wondering if you actually want to make things up with me. And I'm wondering if you need more time because your pride has been hurt. I'm also wondering if maybe you actually hate my guts—in which case I'm wondering what I'm doing here."

"Then don't let me keep you," I said haughtily. It's not what I meant to say, but it's what came out.

Ron stared at me, wondering if I meant it. When I didn't take it back, he said, "I won't be leaving for a few days. If you change your mind about anything, let me know." Then he took a ten-dollar bill from his wallet and placed it on the table.

"Hold it," I told him. "How come you have money all of a sudden? When you were pretending to be Cameron Cavendish you never had a dime."

"I never pretended to be anyone," he argued. "I was broke because I was waiting for my monthly allowance."

"A monthly allowance?" I asked snidely. "How nice."

Ron sighed. "Okay, I guess everything about me gets on your nerves. Maybe I'd better go."

166

"Maybe you had," I said, "but don't bother with the check. It's on me."

He slammed the coffee cup down on top of the ten dollars. "Then consider this the tip!" he shouted. "Good-bye, Molly."

I didn't say anything.

That night I stared at the phone, hoping Ron would call me. If only he'd persisted a little longer in Angela's, I would've given in and made up with him. But now the ball was in my court, and I couldn't bring myself to call him. What if I got Mrs. C. on the phone instead? Or even worse, Mrs. Worthington Spratt? Besides, I didn't know what to say to Ron. Instead, I just sat by the phone, willing it to ring.

It finally did. But it wasn't Ron.

"Hi teach, how're you doin'?"

It took me a second to recognize the voice. "Antoine?"

"That's right."

"How are you? Is everything okay?"

A pause. "Monty gave me your number. He said it'd be okay to call."

"Sure. How is he?"

"Okay."

"Are you sure? Is everything good with you guys?"

"Sure it is."

"How's Sonja? Is she all right?"

"She's okay. She still don't come downstairs but she's okay."

The more Antoine kept insisting everything was

okay, the more I grew worried. "I'm glad you called. What's on your mind?"

Another pause. "I was wonderin' if maybe you'd come around."

I checked my watch. It was after eleven. "Tonight?"

"Yeah, I was wonderin'."

"Antoine, what's wrong? Why do you want me to come there so late?"

"Hey, it don't have to be now. I just figured maybe, that's all."

"Why? What happened?"

"It's about Mitchell. I figured you'd wanna know."

My heart sank. "What about Mitchell? Did something happen to him?"

"I dunno. I think maybe he's gone."

"Gone where?"

"I dunno."

"What happened?"

"There was some shooting around here."

"My God, has Mitchell been shot? Where is he, in the hospital?"

"No, it ain't Mitchell what got shot. But he's gone, and I figured you'd wanna know, that's all."

"I'll be right down," I told him.

# Eighteen

M om was at a movie so I left her a note saying I'd gone out for coffee with a friend. Because it was so late, I debated about taking a taxi but decided the subway would be quicker.

There were heavy vibes in the air. On the subway, the air conditioning conked out. One of the panhandlers working the cars went nuts and started ripping off his clothes. At Forty-second Street, two transit cops hauled the guy away.

The air outside on the street was heavy and oppressive—tension everywhere. I walked crosstown. Beneath the streetlights were several opened hydrants with kids playing in the spray. I hurried along, Mitchell's name pounding in my head. Mitchell, what was wrong with Mitchell?

As I passed Twenty-eighth Street and Park Avenue, I saw a small boy, about seven years old. He was straddling the guardrail of the subway station and singing into his fist, a James Brown screech in his voice and a wild, spaced-out look in his eyes. "Sock it to ya, shake your thinnnggg." He swiveled his hips and wrenched his shoulders forward. "I'm gonna tell ya, shock it to ya, momma, shake your thinnnggg." When a woman walked by, he grabbed her rear end. "Shake your thinnnggg," he yelled. She turned and cursed him out, and the boy cursed back. "Don't mess with me, momma, 'cause I'm a little big man from the Prince George. That's right, I'm a *wild man!*"

The stoop of the Prince George was crawling with people who'd exchanged the heat inside for the heat outside. Mothers sat along the curb barely watching their kids crawl in the gutter. Some guys hung in corners making drug deals. As I walked by them, an old man seated on a folding chair by the entrance grinned at me. He was wearing a white suit and a large white Panama hat. "Welcome to our welfare hellhole," he said. Fanning himself with a newspaper, he laughed out loud.

The lobby looked dirtier and smelled worse than usual. Antoine was waiting for me by the clerk's desk.

"Tell me what happened," I said. "Who got shot?"

Antoine backed off, seeing how worried I was. "Shit, maybe I shouldn't have called. None of this got nothin' to do with me. No way."

"I know that," I assured him. "Please tell me who got shot."

"It was Mitchell's old lady what got shot."

"Mitchell's mother? What happened? Is she all right?"

"She's dead," Antoine said. "It happened a couple nights ago."

I felt a sudden pain in my stomach as if I'd just been punched.

"How did it happen?" I forced myself to ask.

Antoine shrugged. "Some deal was goin' down and it went bad. There was this big shoot-out on the third floor. Mitchell's old lady got caught in the middle. She took a bullet right through the throat. Then the cops come runnin' in. Then the ambulance, but it was too late. When Mitchell got here, they was puttin' Mrs. Crane in one of them big plastic bags. Shit, what a thing to see, ya know? There they was, slidin' her into that bag like she was garbage or somethin'. And her blood all over the place. The cops, they didn't know she was Mitchell's old lady. And he didn't say nothin' about it. I guess he was too scared. Scared they'd take him away, I guess. He just kinda stood there watchin' them load her into the ambulance. But he didn't scream or cry or nothin'. It was weird, man. I asked him after why he didn't say nothin'. He said he didn't wanna be taken away, too. Mitchell ain't got no other family. It was him and his old lady, that's it. Man, he loved her, too. Ya know all that artwork he did when you come? He always brung it to her. She didn't like him hangin' out down here, but she let him whenever you was comin'."

How could such an awful thing happen? Part of me felt like screaming and another part felt like crying.

I'd never even seen Mitchell's mother, but I now

needed to know all I could about her. I asked Antoine to tell me everything, but he knew very little. He said Mrs. Crane had been a cleaning woman. When she couldn't get disability pay after injuring her leg, she went on welfare. Mitchell had no other relatives.

"Why did Mitchell run away?" I asked.

"I guess he figured someone from welfare would be comin' to get him so he cut out. He said not to tell no one and I didn't. But I figured you was different. See, I dunno if Mitchell can handle his self on the street. If maybe he's hangin' out on Forty-second, there's lotsa pimps hang out there, waitin' for us kids. Me, I don't mess with that shit 'cause I don't want no guys screwin' around with me, don't matter how much dough they got. But Mitchell don't know the score as good as me."

"So you think Mitchell is living on the street?"

"Sure, where else? Some kids, they handle it okay. But I dunno about him." As we talked, the crazy kid I'd seen earlier wandered into the lobby. "Take Jermaine over there," Mitchell explained. "He knows the street. To him, it's cool city, understand?"

"But he's so young. What's he on, anyway?"

Antoine shook his head. "He's all cracked up, man. We don't mess with him, he's crazy. He was born in a crack house. He ate a whole pot of crack when he was two years old. His old lady was cookin' it up on the stove, and Jermaine, he thought it was sugar. Yeah, he's a real wild man."

"That's awful," I said, staring at Jermaine. "Listen, I think I should try to find Mitchell. What do you think?"

Antoine shrugged. "It's gonna be hard. Those streets, they eat you up, ya know? If you see him, don't tell him I told you nothin'."

"I won't, I promise. Thanks for telling me, though."

Antoine hiked up his jeans with a macho gesture. "Sure, no sweat. Listen, I gotta go now."

"Wait," I said, remembering what Sonja had said about Antoine's breakdown. "How about you? Are you okay? How're you handling all this?"

Antoine kicked the ground. "Hey, I'm on top of things, ya know? I take care of myself. So long, teach."

As Antoine walked away, I remembered the first time I'd seen him, picking up crack vials in the street. I felt the grimy walls of the Prince George closing in on me, and I hurried out of there.

I had to find Mitchell. I took the subway to Forty-second Street, thinking my best bet would be to check at Covenant House, the shelter for runaway kids near Times Square. They help thousands of runaways each year. I was hoping Mitchell might've gone there. When I arrived, a teenage girl was waiting in the office. She looked hungry, scared, and tired. She sat chain-smoking as a counselor tried to get her family in South Carolina on the phone.

"They don't wanna talk to me, I betcha," said the girl. "My momma, she's the one what kicked me out."

"Hang in there," said the counselor, "we'll get in touch, don't worry."

I introduced myself to the counselor, Miss Ruben. She was a chubby woman with a tired expression but an open, friendly face. I told her about Mitchell, hoping she'd heard something.

"Mitchell Crane? No, I'm sorry. Mainly, we get out-of-towners here—kids off the buses from all over. Or else they come in after they've been hustling for a few months, and they've had it. By then they're anxious to get home. But at first, kids think they can make it on their own. Lots of them try to tough it out."

"Where would he go?" I asked.

"Some congregate in squats—the condemned buildings. There's a whole colony of runaways in each one. Nomad kids escaping prefoster limbo. There are not enough squats for all of them, so some sleep on subways or in bus terminals. If he shows up here and he's an orphan, we'll try to convince him to report to a child protection agency. They'll place him in temporary foster care."

I wrote down my name and phone number. "Please let me know if he shows up, okay? I want to help if I can."

"Sure," said Miss Ruben. "These kids need all the help they can get."

When I left, the teenage girl was still chain-smoking and still hoping to contact her parents.

The thought of Mitchell out on the street with no place to sleep made me sick. Did he have any money? How would he eat? I couldn't go home until I'd found out. But first I had to call Mom so she wouldn't worry.

"Hi, how was the movie?" I asked.

"Pretty good. Where are you? Still having coffee?"

"That's right," I said. "I'll be later than I thought, so don't wait up."

I walked around for almost two hours. I passed the pimps, pushers, and homeless, the hustlers hawking phony Gucci watches, the rip-off three-card monte players, and the tired old men passing out flyers to massage parlors and peep shows.

I passed lots of kids on the street, too. I'd never noticed them before—the ones out all alone at night—the drifters and runaways. Had I ignored them like everyone else did? This time I looked at each one of them, hoping I'd see Mitchell. All I saw was lots of young faces looking old, tired, scared, and hopeless.

It was after two A.M. when I got back uptown. I hurried down Riverside Drive, hoping Mom had gone to bed.

When I walked into the lobby, I saw Leonard sitting on the steps beside the elevator, reading a book.

"What are you doing here?" I asked in surprise.

Leonard looked at his watch. "I didn't realize it was so late. Time flies when you're reading Proust."

"But what are you doing here?" I repeated. "Sorry if I sound cranky, I guess I'm exhausted." I sat down on the steps beside him. "To what do I owe the honor? I mean, I assume you're waiting for me. Why didn't you go upstairs?"

"I did. Two hours ago. Your mother said you'd gone out for coffee with someone—that you'd probably be home soon. So I decided to wait."

"How'd you know where I live?" I asked.

Leonard showed me one of the handmade cards I give out to my customers. It says Molly's Mixed Media and has my address on it.

"You once gave me this, remember?" Then he looked at me quizzically. "I assume your coffee companion is also known as Spratt? Is that who you were with tonight?"

So much had happened since my conversation with Ron, it seemed like a hundred years ago. "What? Oh yeah, Ron and I talked."

Leonard nodded. "I was afraid you might. Opening up those avenues of mutual agreement, eh?"

"Not exactly."

He glanced at me hopefully. "Then maybe I won't have to deep-six my master plan."

"What plan?"

"My plan for winning you, natch," he said with a wry grin. "It occurred to me only this evening. Wasn't it foolish to rush off to become a rodent without first discovering if I'd eliminated the competition? If I were to catch you on the rebound, as they say, I'd have to be nearby whilst you were rebounding. Ergo, I am here. So what's the verdict? Are you rebounding or not?"

I sighed. "I don't know what I'm doing."

"C'mon, spare me the suspense," he pleaded. "Underneath this seemingly flip exterior lurk genuine feelings, not to mention intense curiosity. Have you and the Yup patched it up or what?"

"I can't discuss that now," I told him.

"Why not? After all, I'm asking. It's what we don't know that hurts us, don't you think?"

"I guess so," I agreed, thinking of Mitchell, not Leonard. It was what I didn't know about Mitchell that worried me. "Look, I can't talk about it, okay? Something awful happened to Mitchell, one of my kids. Now he's all alone, living out on the street somewhere, and I can't find him."

Leonard's levity switched to concern. "Hey, that's too bad. Have you tried looking for him at Covenant House? Lots of kids go there."

"That's the first place I went," I told him.

"Well, don't give up," he said reassuringly. "Maybe he'll still show up there. And if not, I bet he'll be okay. When I'm performing, I see lots of street kids. They have their own subculture, you know. And they take care of their own."

I didn't think Leonard really believed that, but it was sweet of him to say it. "Thanks, I hope you're right."

He shrugged. "Under the circumstances, I can see talk of romance seems trivial."

"There is no romance," I said. "The truth is, I acted like a dope with Ron earlier this evening."

"How so?"

I leaned against the banister. "Do you really want to hear about it?"

"Shoot."

"Well, I think I was much too hard on him. It's possible I'm not cut out for a traditional male-female relationship. Recently it seems a crazy person has started living inside my head, and I don't like her. . . . Listen, I'm real tired, and I'm sure none of this makes sense."

"Sure it does," Leonard said. "You're nuts about the yutz. That's the part that doesn't make sense. Not when you consider your options."

I began to yawn. "Have you changed your mind about going to Orlando?"

"Permanently? Maybe. But I'll go for the summer. After that, I'll see how the wind blows. So am I being offered a friendship here or what?"

"What? Oh sure, if you'll take it."

"You talked me into it. You know what they say about friendship. Very often it blossoms into romance."

I yawned again. "I refuse to discuss romance. Not tonight." Then I kissed Leonard on the cheek.

"I'll drop you a line from Mickey Mouse City," he told me. "You might want to take a rain check on that romance offer. Think about it."

I nodded, then said good night.

But I didn't want to think about anyone but Mitchell.

Somehow I had to find him.

# Nineteen

For the next few nights, I hung out around Times Square. I never told Mom where I was going, but as it turned out, I was always safe there. The area is constantly crawling with crowds: a steady flow of tourists, shoppers, and gawkers.

The corner of Forty-second Street and Seventh Avenue is permanently staked out by reformed sinners who preach a return to the Bible. One of them is always standing on the corner, microphone in hand, loudly announcing how everyone will burn in hell if they don't repent. Their message carries for blocks.

And in spite of the sleaze on the streets, there's lots of other stuff going on, too. Along with the pimps, prostitutes, pushers, and pornographers, there are people trying to do some honest business with the hamburger joints, coffee shops, pinball machine parlors, clothing and shoe stores, and so on. I checked in all of them and asked the owners to keep an eye out for Mitchell. I gave everyone a small sketch of him I had copied. At first, the shopkeepers looked suspicious. "What's this kid done?" they asked. I explained he hadn't done anything wrong, that he was lonely and frightened and I wanted to help him. "He might come in here panhandling," I said. "If he does, give him this phone number, okay?"

A few of the shopkeepers took me under their wing. They'd hang out on the sidewalk when they saw me on the street. I got to know some of the Korean sketch artists, too. They'd sit outside the restaurants waiting for customers. For five dollars they'd do a quick charcoal sketch.

After the first day of my search, I created a grid map of the area. Then each evening I'd make my rounds. After the theaters let out at eleven o'clock, I'd see the suburbanites rushing to garages toward the safety of their cars to return to the safety of their homes. I'd also see the teenagers in from the suburbs looking for a good time or trouble or both. And I kept checking back at Covenant House, but so far, Miss Ruben hadn't seen Mitchell.

I was about to give up the idea of ever seeing him again. I couldn't keep coming down to Times Square indefinitely. Mom was beginning to think it was strange that I had a date every night. "You've dated more this week than the entire summer," she'd said suspiciously. "Have you met someone special?"

I was getting discouraged.

Then on the fifth night, when I got home, there was a phone call from Antoine.

"Hi teach, I thought you'd like to know somethin'. When Monty was hangin' out last night he seen Mitchell."

"He did?" I asked excitedly. "Where was he?"

"On Forty-sixth and Broadway. He seen him watchin' some Chinese guy draw pictures on the street."

I knew Antoine must mean one of the Korean sketch artists. "Did Monty speak to him?"

"Sure, they rapped. Mitchell said he likes watchin' the guy draw pictures. Maybe he misses your classes, huh?"

"Maybe so. Did Mitchell say where he was staying?"

"No, he cut out pretty fast. Didn't say much."

"Well, thanks for calling to tell me."

"Sure, no sweat."

The next night I couldn't wait to return to Broadway. I was hoping Mitchell might go back to that same spot, so I hung around Forty-sixth Street for an hour. Just as I was about to leave I spotted him. He was panhandling on the corner of Forty-seventh Street. People coming out of a restaurant dropped some money into his paper McDonald's cup.

I hurried over to him. At first when he saw me he looked as if he wanted to run. Then he changed his mind. But he looked nervous as I approached him.

181

"Hi Mitchell, it's good to see you," I said.

"What're you doing here?" he asked suspiciously.

"Nothing much. How have you been?"

"How do you think?" he asked.

I could see how scared and dirty he was. "I know what's happened, and I'm so sorry. Let's go . . ."

"I'm not going anywhere," he said, trying to push me aside.

I knew he was afraid I'd report him to some agency or turn him in. "Look, I don't want to do anything to you. I just want to buy you some food, okay?"

He nodded.

I took Mitchell to a coffee shop and ordered him a double cheeseburger and a glass of milk. As he waited for his food, he looked at me apprehensively.

"I've missed you," I told him. "And I've been real worried about you."

"I can take care of myself," he said.

"On the street? It's not safe for you out here."

"So where am I safe?" he asked. "In some foster home?"

"I guess so. It might take a while to find you a permanent place, but . . ."

"Just leave off, okay? Forget you saw me, understand? I shouldn't have talked to you."

"Why?" I asked. "Why won't you let me help you?"

He stared at me scornfully. "Help? You think that's what I'll get if I go back there? I'll become an overnighter. I know because I did it once when my mom was in the hospital."

"What's an overnighter?" I asked.

"It means you spend all day sitting with a social worker in a field office while they try to get somewhere for you to sleep that night. Lots of times they can't find a place so you sleep there in the office. On the desk."

The waitress brought Mitchell's food, and he quickly began eating. I'd never heard him talk so much before, and I didn't want him to stop. I could tell he had all sorts of feelings bursting to come out. "Do kids really sleep on desks?" I asked.

"Sure, there's always lots of kids there. Worse-off ones than at the Prince George. Anyway, sometimes foster homes are worse than the streets. You heard what happened to Sonja? Stuff like that happens in foster care, too."

"That's awful," I told him, "but if you stay on the street you can't go to school."

Mitchell looked at me with disgust. "Overnighters don't go to school. They spend their time in offices or on buses. They don't wash, they don't get clean clothes. It's no better than the street."

"The child protection system should help you," I told him.

Mitchell swallowed the last bite of his burger. "That's how the system works," he said matter-of-factly. "Can I have some more food?"

"Sure," I said. I ordered him another burger plus a slice of chocolate cake. It really depressed me that Mitchell's experience had taught him to expect absolutely nothing from anyone. "I'll bet there are lots of people who'd like to help you, just like I would."

"I'm doing okay," he said. "Me and some other guys have moved into a squat."

"The kids at the Prince George miss you. Why don't you come back to art class?"

"What for? That's no good to me now."

"But you're so talented. If you worked at it, maybe someday you could make money doing art. Don't you think that's important?"

Mitchell shrugged. "I don't know." The waitress returned with more food, and Mitchell resumed eating.

"You like to watch the sketch artists on the street, don't you? They make money drawing. Wouldn't you like to do that, too?"

"Maybe. But I don't have any stuff."

"I could get you the art supplies, whatever you need. And I could keep giving you lessons, too. If not with the other kids, it could just be you and me."

"Forget it," he said, hurriedly gobbling down the rest of his burger.

I could tell Mitchell was getting nervous, maybe even suspicious of me. I didn't want him to think I was trying to lure him into the clutches of some social agency. And yet, I wanted to keep some connection going: a bridge he could cross whenever he was ready. "Have you heard of Covenant House? Do you know where it is?"

"Sure," he said, shoving the cake into his mouth. "I can't talk anymore. I've gotta go."

He was beginning to look like a trapped animal. "Wait," I said, pulling out one of my cards. "Take this."

"What for?"

"Just in case you ever want to reach me. I'll leave some art supplies for you at Covenant House. You can pick them up when you like. And call me if you want to, okay?" I looked through my bag. The only extra money I had was a five-dollar bill. "Take this, too," I said.

Mitchell shoved the money and the card into his back pocket. He drank down the last of his milk then wiped his lips with the back of his hand. It was such a little boy gesture, it made me want to cry. "Won't you please tell me where you're staying?" I asked him.

"That's none of your business," he said defiantly. "And don't follow me."

"Will you think over what I told you?" I asked. "About art lessons?"

"Maybe," he said.

Then he hurried out of the coffee shop and disappeared into the crowds on Seventh Avenue.

As I walked home, I felt rotten. Mitchell was probably right: the child protection system did stink. He should know—it hadn't worked for him. What kind of crappy world is it where a kid thinks he's better off on the street?

And what about me? What had I thought I could do for Mitchell? Had I supposed my finding him would change his life? Who was I kidding?

I was totally confused.

When I got home there was a package for me in the lobby. I took it upstairs. Mom was already asleep. She had been spending all her free time practicing her old numbers, and now she was lying in bed with piles of sheet music scattered across her chest. I picked everything up, then covered her with a blanket.

I went into the kitchen and opened the package. It was a book from Ron—*Letters of E. B. White*. And it had an inscription: To Molly, They say reading someone's letters is like listening to their heartbeat. With affection, Ron.

His note made me want to cry, it was so sweet. I fixed myself a cup of tea, sat in the kitchen, and read the note over and over again. Then I picked up the phone and called him.

"Hi, it's Molly. I hope I'm not calling too late. I got your present, and I wanted to say thanks."

"It's not too late," he said, "and you're welcome."

"When did you stop by?" I asked.

"Earlier this evening. No one was there so I left the package in the lobby."

"I'm sorry I missed seeing you," I told him. "And I love your inscription."

"It's not mine exactly, but I agree with the sentiment."

"So do I," I said. Then I didn't know what else to say.

For a moment, Ron didn't know either, I guess. Then after a while he asked, "Can we see each other, Molly? I really miss you."

"Sure."

"Good. I'm leaving for East Hampton in the morning. Come for the weekend? We have lots of room."

"I know," I said, "ten of them."

186

"How about it?"

"What would we do out there?" I asked. "Swim together in the pool?"

"If you like. We'll do whatever you want. Will you come? We'd have a great weekend together."

"Would we?" I got a mental picture of old Franciepoo bobbing up and down right next to me in the Spratt pool. "I don't think so."

"Why not?"

"I'd probably be more at home in the sea lion tank," I joked.

"Quit it, Molly. Come on."

"Nope, it's not for me. I'd use the wrong fork or something and mortify everyone."

"Cut the bull. Why won't you come? You said you didn't know me and we'd need to get acquainted. So let's start. Or was that bull, too?"

I didn't answer him right away. I envisioned Ron's ten-room house in the Hamptons and his spacious apartment overlooking Central Park with that empty room used only for ironing. Then I saw Mitchell squatting in some wretched abandoned building. I knew one had nothing to do with the other, but I couldn't help making the connection.

"Well, are you going to tell me the real reason you won't come?" Ron asked.

"I'm not sure. Maybe it's me who I need to get acquainted with, not you."

"What's that mean?"

"I'm still angry at you. Maybe because you have tons of money and a pool and all sorts of things when so many people have nothing. I don't like feeling like this, but I do. Does that sound crazy?"

"Sort of," said Ron. "And yet, it doesn't. At least not altogether."

"Things have really fallen apart for my kids," I told him. "First there was Sonja. Now Mitchell is living on the street."

"Oh, I see," he said. "No, I don't. Not really. I'm sorry to hear about Mitchell, but I don't understand why you won't see me."

"Look, I was joking before, but it's true. I'd embarrass you if I came to your Hampton house. I'd probably strong-arm your parents into giving me money to help kids like Mitchell."

"What's wrong with that? If it's a worthy cause, I'm sure my parents might help. Would you like me to ask them?"

"No. Don't you get it? First, I get mad at you for being from a rich family. Then I get jealous. Then I expect their money. It's all screwy!"

"No it's not, Molly. Anyway, who said you had to solve the world's problems all by yourself? Don't you realize you always refer to those kids as *yours*? They're not your exclusive responsibility. Why not let other people help, too? I don't guarantee my parents are the ones who'll do it, but . . ."

"It's more complicated than that," I protested. "Don't you see? I don't know how I really feel about anything! Except that I'd definitely feel funny going to the Hamptons right now. So let's leave it at that, okay? We'll see each other when you get back."

"We can't," said Ron. "I'm leaving for Paris after that."

"Paris? How come?"

"I finally decided on my major. I'm doing my junior year at the Sorbonne, where I'll study architecture. Thanks to you. It was after we had that conversation at the Met I realized how much it excited me."

"I thought *I* had excited you," I said teasingly.

"I mean intellectually excited. Of course, the idea has been floating around in my head for a while, but I needed some verification. Maybe I'll dig up some truly obscure female architect so you can throw her name around at a Guerrilla Girls meeting. Do they have meetings?"

"I don't think so. Isn't this all a little sudden?" I asked him. "Switching schools takes lots of planning, doesn't it?"

"Usually, but Dad pulled some strings and cut through the red tape." Ron paused then added, "Isn't this the appropriate time for you to make some comment about rich fat cats?"

"No, I don't think so."

"Well, now that you know I'm leaving, won't you reconsider and come visit?"

"Now that I know you're leaving, I want to. But I don't think I will."

"Why not?"

"I need more time." I knew that somehow I'd mixed Ron up with his family, his money, Mitchell's problems, and my own desire to make some social statement. I'd need time to unravel the whole mess. Plus I wanted to be around in case Mitchell *did* call. "I think maybe we should put things on hold for a while. Don't you?"

"No, obviously I don't. Do we have a relationship or not? Do you want one?"

"I'm trying to explain that I'm confused about the relationship. Not emotionally and physically, that's real clear. But economically and socially it's still real fuzzy. I'm having big problems there. You know?" Ron didn't answer. "Or maybe you don't think I'm worth waiting for, is that it?"

I could hear Ron sigh, and then he began to laugh. "I'm sure I'll never meet anyone like you again, Molly. You don't make a damn bit of sense, but I think you're terrific. So where does that leave us?"

"Maybe with something real good in the future?"

"Why can't it be now?"

"I'll be too busy. Really. I've got lots of work in the city."

"Are you sure I can't change your mind?"

"No, I'm not sure. But I'd rather you didn't try."

"Okay, but if *you* change your mind give me a call. A month is an awfully long time."

# Twenty

The summer is over. Remember those compositions everyone had to write in grammar school? . . . "What I Did on My Summer Vacation." If I had to write one now, I wouldn't know where to start. I can't believe it's such a short time since my argument with Isaac about his stupid prom. So much has happened since then.

At the beginning of August, I thought about Ron constantly. He kept telephoning. We'd talk. He'd say I was immovable, intransigent, and obstinate. He swore I was the most stubborn redhead in the world. And he kept insisting I change my mind about visiting him in the Hamptons. I kept refusing. I still felt there were lots of things I had to work out first. And I was right.

I haven't seen Mitchell again. The day after our talk,

I dropped off some art supplies for him at Covenant House. Two days later, Miss Ruben called to tell me Mitchell had stopped by and picked them up. I was so pleased, I delivered another bunch of supplies the next day. The following week, Mitchell stopped by again. When he showed up the second time, Miss Ruben tried to get him to reveal where he was living. He refused. But I'm not giving up hope. I won't let Mitchell become like some street kids who close off to the rest of the world. If I can keep in contact with him, maybe I'll break through his armor eventually. As long as Mitchell wants art supplies, we have a connection. So I'll keep leaving packages for him. Sometimes I include food, too. And notes. And money whenever I can.

Last week I got a call from Mr. Morales. He managed to have Sonja's family be among the first ones phased out of the Prince George. And maybe they'll get permanent housing in the Bronx soon.

"We've been working on that hotel for a long time," he explained. "We were hoping that by next year most of the families would be relocated. But with all the budget cuts, that probably won't happen now."

"How about therapy?" I asked him.

"Sonja is on a waiting list," he said, "but don't hold your breath on that one, either. It'll take a long time."

For a while there'll still be lots of kids living at the Prince George, and they're all keeping me real busy. I organized a new group. I have sixteen students. During August, I gave them lessons twice a week. When I return to school, I'll have to cut back, but we're on a roll. Antoine and Darryl stop by sometimes, and I'm hoping Mitchell might return, too. In my last package, I left a note reminding him about our classes. You never know, right?

I've been getting notes, too. One day I received three postcards all at once: from Leonard, Isaac, and Ron. You should've heard Mom carry on when she picked up the mail. "So many young men in your life, Molly. Have I met them all?"

I figured it was time to come clean. "One is a street performer who turned into Mickey Mouse. The other is a millionaire."

I don't think she believed me.

Isaac's postcard is of the Trevi Fountain. He says:

Meeting lots of fiery Italian females. They're all *magnifico,* but none has fiery red hair like yours.

Leonard sent me a postcard showing Disney World. He wrote:

Getting into the swing of being Mickey Mouse but I miss my alter ego, Rempha—not to mention someone else. I fear I can't hang in for the long rodent haul, so maybe it's back to the gold greasepaint pretty soon.

On Ron's postcard, there's a photo of one of those Hampton windmills near the beach. It says:

As I walk the beach and stare out to sea, all my thoughts are of you. And when flotsam washes to shore, I think of your collages. Take pity. Come visit.

I liked knowing Ron was missing me. And I liked the pleasurable pain of missing him, too. For the moment, our missing one another seemed much less complicated than our being together. Especially since I knew I had lots of work to do before we met again. I'd suddenly grown too busy to think much about my missing him.

Mom is real busy, too. She's still teaching piano during the day, but starting next month she'll have a gig on Saturday nights, playing piano bar in an East Side restaurant. She'll be on trial the first two weeks, but if she's a hit, she'll become permanent three nights a week. That means Mom can finally drop a day or two of her teaching. She's thrilled. Every chance she gets, she rehearses. I often hear her in the living room, polishing up her old theme song, "I Ain't Down Yet."

Her voice still sounds a little rusty to me, but maybe that's what gives it character. And even if she's older, she's got style. That's exactly what the restaurant owner told her: "Too many younger performers don't have style." Mom can't wait to slip into her slinky satin Rita Hayworth costume again. And I can't wait, either. This time, I'll be her biggest fan. After all, performing is what Mom really loves.

I'm doing what I love, too. In fact, I'm beginning to think Mom's theme song should also be mine because I just finished my most ambitious, exciting art project. I call it *Vicious Circles*. In three connecting circular panels, I outlined the lives of the kids who live in the Prince George Hotel. In the center circle I painted portraits of all my kids, and I've tried to capture each one's uniqueness. On one side panel I included newspaper clippings, photos, budget stats, etc.—all of which illustrate how they've been trapped within the system. Twelve hundred kids in the Prince George alone! And there are lots more hotels like it. The city spends over twenty-five thousand dollars per family to house welfare clients in those rotten hellholes.

On the other side I included examples of the kids' artwork. Lots of them have talent, and they desperately want a chance to shine. It's a powerful statement, and I'm proud of it.

I'm also proud of the way all my kids worked together. When I explained their drawings would be part of something I'd show to art galleries, they got real excited. They all doubled their efforts—cooperating, helping one another. More than ever, I realized what a positive force art lessons bring into their lives. I began to wonder what it would be like if I could teach them art every day. If not me, then someone else, maybe. Just like Ron said, they weren't only *my* kids. Sure, other people could help, too. I knew I could get other art students to volunteer. Maybe we could set up something so the kids could get lessons every day. If only we had a more adequate area than the dirty floor of the Prince George lobby: a clean, safe space for kids to do art.

Once I'd gotten the idea, I couldn't get it out of my head. Was it just a fantasy? Maybe not. After all, I thought swimming with sea lions was only a fantasy, but Ron Spratt had made it happen.

The idea stayed stuck in my mind, so I decided to

flesh it out. A community arts center. What would it take to make that idea come true? I figured all it required to create such a center was money to rent a large space, donations of art supplies, sufficient volunteers, and funding to ensure that once it got started, it would continue. That didn't seem like such a fantasy. Even if it did, maybe someone might help me to fulfill it!

I thought of Lydia Spratt. After all, Ron's mother was a pro at raising money for good causes. And my kids were a terrific cause, not a charity. I wouldn't be asking her for a handout, just to help me get the kids what they deserve.

I was so excited by the idea, I wrote a letter to her, asking for help raising funds for the project. I outlined all my ideas. I took some photos of *Vicious Circles* and I included the snapshots with my proposal. And then I let the whole thing lie on my desk several days. I couldn't bring myself to mail it. What if Mrs. Spratt remembered me from the museum? The girl who had thought Ron was the housekeeper's son. Eventually, I swallowed my pride and sent the letter.

And then I waited. It was the end of August, so I knew the Spratts would soon be returning from the Hamptons.

Two days after Labor Day I got a phone call.

"Miss Malone? This is Lydia Spratt. I received your letter."

"You did?" I asked stupidly. I hadn't expected her to call me. I figured a note, maybe. "What did you think of it?" I asked, hearing my voice start to squeak.

196

"I think an art center for homeless children is a commendable idea. Personally, I've never raised money for small groups, only large organizations."

I braced myself for a polite turndown. "Does that mean you're not interested?"

"I'd like to learn more about your project. As I understand it, you plan to have art students volunteer their services at this center."

"Yes, that's right."

"Mightn't it be difficult to get their commitment?"

"Maybe, but I don't think so. I know lots of students who'd probably love to help."

"I see. Would you personally supervise this center?"

"Me?" I asked, unprepared for her question. "Naturally I'd be there as a volunteer, but—well, I guess I haven't thought about that part yet," I admitted.

"All new ventures have unforeseen elements," Mrs. Spratt noted. "I've learned that nothing is as simple as it first appears. For instance, you may also need salaried employees. A community arts center shouldn't depend exclusively on volunteers."

"No, I suppose not," I agreed. I felt she was definitely interested in the project. Mrs. Spratt sounded real efficient, but I must've sounded idiotic. I was still surprised she'd called me. "Yes, I guess you're right. We'll need to hire some art teachers. Although we might get teachers to volunteer, too. These kids are so terrific, Mrs. Spratt. They're eager to learn, and lots of them are really talented. I bet teachers would love to donate their time to them."

"Perhaps we should meet to discuss the whole thing in detail," she suggested.

"You want us to meet?" I clearly hadn't thought things out fully. What had I expected her to do? Send me a check? Give me a black-tie dinner at the Metropolitan? "You and me?" I asked densely.

"Yes, that's right."

I still wasn't sure Mrs. Spratt knew who I was, so I decided to tell her. Confused identities had caused enough trouble in my life lately. "Sure, we can meet. But I hope things turn out better than the first time."

There was a pause. "I didn't know we had already met," she confessed. "I'm afraid I don't remember."

I envisioned myself wearing that serving wench outfit, and Mrs. Spratt in her cabochon emeralds. "It was at the Metropolitan Museum benefit. I was your waitress. I served you fish."

Another pause. I wasn't sure what to expect next. Would she hang up on me? Maybe the whole deal was becoming embarrassing.

"Oh," she finally replied. "I thought your name sounded familiar. Yes, I'm sorry. You're Ron's friend. Did you two ever straighten out that confusion? I didn't quite understand it."

Mrs. Spratt acted like it didn't matter. Was I the only one who'd given it importance? "Neither did I," I confessed. "And yes, we straightened it all out."

"That's good. I was dreadfully nervous that night. Benefits always make me nervous."

"Me too, I guess," I told her.

"Yes. Well, about our meeting, could you come here next Thursday morning at ten o'clock?"

"Sure," I said. Then I suddenly remembered I'd be back in school then. "No, wait, I can't. How about Thursday at four?"

"Four o'clock Thursday? Yes, that's fine. Your proposal sounds very exciting. We'll have lots to talk about. I hope I can help you make your arts center become a reality. I'd like to try. We'll discuss everything at our meeting."

*Our* meeting? Was this going to become *our* project? I hoped so. "Yes, thank you, Mrs. Spratt."

"You're welcome. Good-bye, Miss Malone."

When I hung up, I felt so light-headed I thought I'd float away. Lydia Spratt actually sounded nice. Not at all snooty, just nice. Why should that astound me? After all, Ron was nice, wasn't he? I was still in a daze when I went down to check the mailbox. In it, I found a letter from Ron. From Paris!

Dear Molly,

I endured our August separation because I'd promised you time to work things out. Have you? I hope so. You never mentioned September, though. I had planned to slink back into the city, laden with champagne (do you drink it—ever?) and roses (or do you prefer wildflowers?) and have one memorable dinner together (do you like French, Cajun, Italian, what?) before I left for France. Unfortunately, there were major glitches and I had to leave early. I've been here three days, but I still haven't waded through all the confusion. (I was mistakenly registered as a philosophy major!)

So far, I've had no fun, just thinking of you all

199

the time. (That's not meant the way it sounds.) I can't enjoy Paris alone, knowing how much we'd enjoy it together. Please let me buy you a ticket to come over. Or else I can arrange a cheap charter fare that you can pay for. How about it? You can stay with friends of my family. (Relax, they don't have a pool.) I've decided you're definitely worth waiting for, but I'd rather not wait forever. So if you don't come, I'll fly back to the States during school break. Let me know. As Stuart Little said, "I shall await your arrival with all the eagerness I can muster." So why not head north (northeast, actually), just like Stuart did in his search for Margalo? Please come. I'm running out of E. B. White quotes.

Love, Ron

As I rode up in the elevator, I reread the letter. Paris with Ron. I pictured us strolling along the Left Bank together, stopping for café au lait in a charming bistro, taking moonlight walks along the Seine, touring the Louvre and having magnificent arguments about every painting. Were *all* my dreams about to come true?

No, not quite all of them. I thought of Mitchell and suddenly I dropped back to reality. I still didn't know where Mitchell was living. I decided it was time to put together another package of supplies for him.

I went into the M.R. and assembled colored markers, a sketch pad, and a box of charcoal. I included some food I'd bought: cookies, peanuts, raisins, and crackers.

Where was his squat? I wondered. How did he

spend the days? Did he ever take his art supplies into the park to sketch the scenery? Did he ever visit the museums?

I browsed through my file and found a floor plan of the Metropolitan Museum. I circled a few of the galleries I thought Mitchell would like to see, taped a couple of pennies onto it, and then stuffed it into the box with a note:

Dear Mitchell,

You can get into this museum for only a penny. And you can stay there all day. If you visit, I hope you let me know what paintings you like best. If you go on Saturday, you'll see me outside on the side-walk. That's where I sell my artwork. Take care of yourself. I miss you.

Molly

Then I answered Ron's letter.

Dear Ron,

Paris during school break sounds like a terrific idea. (Never mind the charter flight, a courier deal will be even cheaper.) By then, I hope to have lots of surprises to share with you. I think you may be meeting a totally different person (although I'm still just as bossy and stubborn). I've learned that things I thought were important really aren't, and some things I thought were almost impossible aren't at all. Does that make sense? Maybe not, but I can explain it in detail when we see each other. And until we meet, remember what else Stuart said: — "a person who is looking for something doesn't travel very fast." So I'll be enjoying the rest of the wait.

Love, Molly

I dropped my letter to Ron into the mail, then I delivered my package for Mitchell to Covenant House. On the way back home, I walked up Broadway. As I passed Eighty-sixth Street, I saw the remnants of Hani's Sistine Chapel painting on the sidewalk. The brilliant top colors have already washed away. But the denser colors of the base coat are still sticking to the cement. Those foundation colors are always the most important.

I stared into the giant eyes of the Delphic Sybil and I felt very happy. Like Stuart, I felt I was finally headed in the right direction.